MORVERN CALLAR

Alan Warner was born in Oban, Argyll, and lives in Dublin. *Morvern Callar*, his first novel, won a Somerset Maugham Award. He is also the author of *These Demented Lands*, winner of the 1998 Encore Award, *The Sopranos*, which won the Saltire Scottish Book of the Year Award, and most recently, *The Man Who Walks*.

ALSO BY ALAN WARNER

These Demented Lands
The Sopranos
The Man Who Walks

Alan Warner

MORVERN CALLAR

V

VINTAGE

Published by Vintage 2002

1 3 5 7 9 10 8 6 4 2

First published in Great Britain by
Jonathan Cape Ltd, 1995
First published by Vintage in 1996

VINTAGE
Random House, 20 Vauxhall Bridge Road, London SW1V 2SA

Random House Australia (Pty) Limited
20 Alfred Street, Milsons Point, Sydney
New South Wales 2061, Australia

Random House New Zealand Limited
18 Poland Road, Glenfield,
Auckland 10, New Zealand

Random House (Pty) Limited
Endulini, 5a Jubilee Road, Parktown 2193, South Africa

The Random House Group Limited Reg. No. 954009

www.randomhouse.co.uk

A CIP catalogue record for this book
is available from the British Library

ISBN 0 09 944994 3

Papers used by Random House
are natural, recyclable products made from wood grown in
sustainable forests. The manufacturing processes conform to
the environmental regulations of the country of origin

Printed and bound in Great Britain by
Cox & Wyman Ltd, Reading, Berkshire

This novel: for Heather Black, for Holger Czukay and Peter Brötzmann. For Duncan McLean and remembering G. Cunningham (1965–1989).

Mr Clay in the same hesitating manner told him that he had in mind books and accounts, not of deals and bargains, but of other things which people at times had put down, and which other people did at times read. The clerk reflected on this matter and repeated, no, he had never heard of such books.

Isak Dinesen, The Immortal Story

Hᴇ'ᴅ ᴄᴜᴛ His throat with the knife. He'd near chopped off His hand with the meat cleaver. He couldnt object so I lit a Silk Cut. A sort of wave of something was going across me. There was fright but I'd daydreamed how I'd be.

He was bare and dead face-down on the scullery lino with blood round. The Christmas tree lights were on then off. You could change the speed those ones flashed at. Over and over you saw Him stretched out then the pitch dark with His computer screen still on.

I started the greeting on account of all the presents under our tree and Him dead. Useless little presents always made me sad. I start for me then move on to everybody when I greet about the sad things. Her from Corran Road with all sons drowned off the boats. She bubbled till she lost an eye. I greeted in heaves and my nose was running.

I dropped the Silk Cut and it burned to the filter on a varnished floorboard. I stopped the greeting cause I couldnt breathe and was perished cold. I slowed down the speed of the flashing Christmas tree lights. I put on the scullery light then the immersion heater then the bar fire but I didnt put a record on.

I supposed I was stewing over going out to the box by the garage to phone police or ambulance or whoever took things to the next stage. Then all in the port would know. They'd print a photo in the paper. His old dad who lived away in a country would have to be told. My fosterdad and the railway and all in the superstore would know.

That immersion heater took a half hour and it was eightish on the video. I needed to boil the kettle to get the mess offof my face, what with the greeting and that.

I couldnt get past Him without stepping in His blood and I was scared to go too nearish so's I got my things in the bedroom. I took the last pill in that cycle.

I came back towards the scullery then took a running jump over the dead body. The sink was full of dishes so I had to give them all a good rinse. The face was by my bare foot. I fitted the kettle spout under the tap. Then I put my underwear over the spout and tugged the elastic round the sides. When the kettle boiled I put the warm knickies on. I jumped back over Him ready to throw the kettle away, after all you don't want to scald your legs. My foot came down in blood. I stepped forward and swore out loud. I wiped my foot on the rug.

I washed my face in the sort of burnt-smell kettle water then I needed toilet.

Sitting there I saw I'd locked the door even though He was dead. I did a number-one then a number-two remembering always to wipe backwards. Though He was dead I used the air freshener spray.

For sake of something to do I tidied away all the presents for Him, Red Hanna, Vanessa the Depresser and Lanna into the boiler cupboard. I lit a Silk Cut. I lined up the presents from Him to me then just tore them all open one after another like apple boxes at the work: a polished steerhide jacket, a packet of yellowish low denier stockings, a lighter that looked goldish, a basque thing all silky and a dear-looking Walkman with batteries in. I started to greet again as I stepped in the blood and knelt. I ended up touching His hair cause the rest was cold. All floor-blood had a sort of skin on. When I saw it burnt down I pushed the Silk Cut butt in the blood and it hissed snubbing out.

I'd been greeting so long the water would be hot. Bits of the blood-skin hung from my legs when I stood up and fresh drops came off. My bare feet left blackish foot-prints across the floorboards. I wiped the footprints into smears with the shiny Christmas wrapping paper.

I kneeled in the bath. I washed my knees and legs and in me. I got my legs warm so there were no goosebumps then shaved them and that. I gave my shin a wee nick with the razor and blood lifted in a bubble then trickled quick. I put in a splash of the bubblebath and filled the tub. The water was too burny so I put in cold.

The flat had warmed up and was quite cosy. I used every clean towel on me. In the bedroom I used moisturiser all over and put the knickies back on. I adjusted the straps on the new basque thing and buttoned up a long shirt over it. I used a touch of Perfect Plum Glimmerstix and Raspberry Dream powder blush then did my lips with Unsurpassed Wine. When I held the tissue taut to take the excess off the paper ripped, so I did a deep breath and used another. My nails were in a state as per usual so I sat blowing on them after putting a little more Dusky Cherry on.

I tied the reddish scarf into my hair and put the greenish socks on. I was stewing over the yellowy stockings under the velvet trousers which feel quite rampant, or the jeans with the knees out and all the slashes up the back to the bum with tights under. I plumped for *just* the velvet trousers. I laced on the baseball boots and used the goldish lighter on a Silk Cut. When I put the steerhide jacket on it had a smell and creaked as you moved the arms. I put the Walkman in the pocket and the plugs in my ears after fitting the long ear-rings on. I took some cassettes: new ambient, queer jazzish, darkside hardcore and that C60 I'd made with Pablo Casals doing Nana on his cello again and again.

I sat on the toilet with the door locked listening to all the stuff on the Walkman; the Auto-Reverse turned the cassettes without having to take them out! I tried the goldish lighter on Silk Cuts. Every now and then I lifted the toilet seat to drop the butts in.

When I came out, the video showed twelvish. Everyone who was going to work from down the stair would have gone so there would be less chance of nosey-parkers when the ambulance or police came to take Him away.

4

On the computer screen was:

NOTE ON THE DISC

XXXX

I pressed the diddleypush to eject the floppy disc after Z&Y-ing the keyboard then I pulled out the plug. I put the disc in the jacket pocket. I grabbed two packs of Silk Cut out the carton and put some of the cassettes in the jacket pockets. I switched off Christmas tree lights, fire and immersion heater then counted the change in my purse for phoning police or ambulance or whoever, from the box by the garage. I wasnt going to have enough till payday. On the mat was a catalogue from a model shop in the south. I chucked it in the bin, locked up careful then moved down the stair past the doors of other flats.

Out there were no people. Puddles were frozen and wee-ones off from school had burst all ice. A car passed and you saw smoke clinging round the exhaust. Miles Davis doing He Loved Him Madly offof Get Up With It was going in the ears. My hands were in the jacket pockets, the nose was cold like it was pinched between finger and thumb; I touched the computer disc in the other pocket, as I walked up to the phonebox I felt the cassette moving next to one pinkie, and it was that bit where the trumpet comes in for the second time: I walked right past the phonebox. It was the feeling the music gave that made me.

It was a dead clear freezing day with blueish sky the silvery sun and you saw all breath. I walked by the

Phoenix and the Bayview. Across the bay between the walls of St John's and Video Rental you saw snow on the mountains of the island where my fostermother lay buried. Along at the seawall people were crossing the road into shops. All cars and buses had smoke showing round the exhaust. A man inside a car moved his hand at me from across the road. I waved back: it was just Ramraider my driving instructor giving a lesson. A fishing boat was coming in with a light on the mast. I stopped and watched the boat pass over to the railway pier. I took a big breath of the bright morning and used the goldish lighter on a Silk Cut.

I changed cassettes to Music Revelation Ensemble at the railway station looking up to see the time. I knew my fosterdad was away down through the pass on the early train so I crossed the square. The Christmas tree with the coloured household bulbs was still switched on. The other phones were there so I walked round the corner the way I had for eight year.

I stopped in the superstore carpark to finish the Silk Cut then when the drums came in after the solo bass on Bodytalk I strode on through the sliding door and up to the signing book. Trust Creeping Jesus to be stood there and he moved his mouth at me. He flicked one of the earplugs out. Youre late by forty-five minutes so get up there, I heard in his south accent. Christ had Christmas already? he says nodding at the steerhide jacket and the Walkman. I put the plug back in my ear and took the door up to the ladies' staffroom.

Lanna from bakery was there lifting her hand to lick round her fingers. They were all sugar from stacking donuts. *Where* did you get the *jacket*? she says. I put it round her shoulders and, touching it, she asked if my boyfriend give it me. She called Him by name. I got my locker key and took out the nylon uniform, the apron, the tights in a ball and the schoolish shoes. When I saw the uniform it nearly made me turn round and tell Lanna He was dead. She was playing with the Walkman, winding forward so you heard Music Revelation Ensemble all far-away-like. Lanna was laying off how bakery had kept her on over five hours without break and there was a law against it. Have you bought all His presents? she says. I nodded and tugged a leg out the velvet trousers then undid the buttons and took off the shirt. You could see the basque thing. I put on the brownish tights and the uniform while Lanna buttoned the neck up and smoothed the nylon onto me with her palms. Then she gently took my earrings out and was biting her lip. You werent allowed jewellery on the section. Why did you go to the fuss of putting these in Morvern? she says. I put the jacket and the Walkman in my locker. Theyre lovely, so is your slip thing, Lanna says, pointing at my chest. Then she goes, since we were off for three day would I come to The Mantrap and get mortal after closedown? She would meet me with a summerbag: shoes and the little black number, though it had a totey hole at the shoulder; I could change in the bogs on the north pier. I nodded, she told me a time and place then showed the half bottle Southern Comfort hid in her locker. She lit a Regal and I took a drag. I nodded. Smiled.

Down the stair the section was pandemonium. Smugslug had gone and let them put too many tatties out on the shelves. Loads had fallen and were getting kicked about by shoppers' feet. I kneeled to pick them up then stepped in and shoved the tatties to the back of the shelves. I could never grow nails on that job: my hands were all soil.

Down the tunnel by the fridges, Smugslug tried to give me hell for lateness. I was too famished and walked away. In the fridge I pinched plums and polished them on my apron. I bit leaning forward so juice dripped on the floor. I loaded a six-wheeler with loose carrots, prepack tomats, icebergs, cos, watercress, loose mushies, prepacks and caps.

Smiler came out the tunnel, empty boxes stacked on his six-wheeler. He started breaking the boxes down for the baler. Going out tonight? he says. I goes, Mmm. He says, Mantrap? I goes, Uh huh.

I pushed my six-wheeler along the tunnel and between shoppers. When I was tipping out the loose carrots by resting the pallet against my thigh then twisting to coup it, Smiler pushed along a six-wheeler stacked taller than me with soft fruit. He shouted to Shadow the shelf-stacker on the next section about the last weekend at The Mantrap.

I took my empty boxes and pallets back to the baler. I

stacked the pallets, put the wooden boxes by the service lift then broke the cardboard ones down, being canny not to slash my hands on the copper staples. I heaved the cardboard in and put it on Crush. When Smiler arrived I handed him the list written on a torn bit of box:

> 3 Delicious
> 3 Grannies
> 2 New Zealand
> Lems loose/prepack
> Oranges dozens + halfs
> Loose garlic
> Avocados

Smiler told about Smugslug and how I shouldve been Section Supervisor. I just looked at him and goes, Mmm, cause with my discipline record and the way Creeping Jesus was browned-off at me I was stuck in that job for ever.

Smiler started stacking full pallets and boxes on his six-wheeler. You knew by the time I had broken his boxes down I would follow on with more veg and soft fruit then he would go over tatties. You kept the section on the ball.

After four hours exact I tanked it up the canteen. I'd used the goldish lighter on a Silk Cut before I was up the stair. I got two rolls and put ketchup in them then sat beside Tequila Sheila from tills.

New jacket, saw you come in with it, she says.

Uh huh, I goes.

What are you doing for Christmas, just going over to Red Hanna's?

Mmm.

Are you on to closedown?

Mmm.

Mantrap?

Uh huh.

Oh well, I'm on. See yous both the night.

Tequila Sheila and me were in that gang on the scheme: The Complex Girls. They stopped talking when I started going about with Him, watching him build the model up in the loft. Cause of tallness I had started part-time with the superstore when thirteen, the year it got built. The superstore turn a blind eye; get as much out you as they can. You ruin your chances at school doing every evening and weekend. The manager has you working all hours cash in hand, no insurance, so when fifteen or sixteen you go full-time at the start of that summer and never go back to school.

Afternoon was as per usual but when section was on the ball, Creeping Jesus had me put on service at The Seacow's till instead of helping Smugslug sort the load that arrived.

At the till I filled plastic carrier bags with Christmas stuff for folk. A woman with a well-to-do south voice told me to wash my soily hands before touching her messages. Some bills came to hundreds of pounds. They all paid with these credit cards. I put the bags in trolleys and pushed them to the Volvos. I had a well-to-do family and their voices. The biggest bill and a trolley just for wine. A daughter my age who looked on while I loaded the boot. No change for a tip cause they used credit card. The husband went, Merry Christmas.

After service me and Smiler let the section run down but Creeping Jesus made us stock up just before the superstore shut so there would be tons to take off after the shoppers left though we werent paid a penny after closedown. I could see Smiler going to go mental so's I nodded him to leave when the voice told the shoppers to go.

The superstore was quiet with most lights out to save electric. That fly devil Creeping Jesus would be in his office with the one-way glass. I knew he would be looking down at me through the mirrors.

I stacked the Delicious in shiny piles. I put all the soft fruit and perishable veg in customer service trolleys then shoved them two at a time down the tunnel into the fridges.

I covered the tatties with sacks to slow down shooting and I swept the section. I washed the shelves, tipping the buckets down the drain in the meat-cutting room. You could see the pale yellowy maggots still there under the grate.

I used to work in the meat. You cleaned up each night. Afterwards you smelled of blood and it was under your nails as you lifted the glass near your nose in the pub.

You pulled the bleeding plastic bag of gubbins, cut open by bones, to the service lift. Blood spoiled three pairs of shoes. You were expected to supply your own footwear.

Up the lockers I put rollon under my oxters and changed. I used the goldish lighter on a Silk Cut. As I was passing Creeping Jesus shouted, Morvern, from his office. Inside he gave me an envelope and stared at me over his beard in that perv way. Merry Christmas, he says. I just switched Music Revelation Ensemble on in the ears and walked out.

In the carpark I opened the letter under a light. I didn't look at words just the overall number of lines on the paper: A lateness letter; a new line had appeared below the usuals and that would say it was a final warning. I tore it into bits then scattered them over the wall into The Black Lynn, the little river that flows under the port.

In the night you could see breath billowing out under streetlight. All with Street Bride going in the ears, I walked into Haddows, took a cheap bottle of wine to the till and counted out most of my money. I walked down the esplanade in front of The Marine and The Saint Columba and the other closed hotels. I held the bottle inside the paper bag to my chest. Boys in cars were circling the port roads. You recognised the same cars again and again and though it was cold the elbows were out.

Though alone I climbed to the circular folly above the

port. I put Can: Delay 1968 in my ears while I used the goldish lighter on Silk Cuts and bolted the wine.

Up there in darkness you could see the lights of the whole port, from The Complex round the back to the piers below, like a model with the small hotels, little lights, circling toy cars and still boats in the bay.

Theres massive floodlights on the south pier where the island ferries tie up by the railway station. Below the folly you see the north pier, the darkened bay, the first island, then the strip of darker sea to the snowy mountains of my fostermother's island where she's buried. Behind The Complex, mountains go east to the Back Settlement, then west through the pass to the village beyond the power station.

I put the empty bottle on the stone of the folly and, for a moment, port lights were gathered in it: I smashed it against the granite circle. Oh Little Star of Bethlehem was in my ears.

Gingerly I walked down Jacob's Ladder, the steep steps on the cliff behind the distillery. White steam from the roof was going straight up in the air so close you could lean out and touch then look up to where the steam vanished. On each platform bench a couple were kissing seriously in the coldness.

Lanna was waiting outside Menzies. She was wearing the short skirt and the bolero jacket with her hair up. Hello Lizzy Long-Stocking, she says lifting a summerbag with the superstore name written off it. Are you mortal? she says. We both went hysterical with laughing. We walked arm in arm to the toilets on the north pier and got in the same cubicle. The Bog Creeper came out her wee bothy so I stood on the toilet seat and Lanna whipped her skirt down to her boots and sat. After the Bog Creeper had gone I sat behind Lanna and without talking we passed the Southern Comfort back and forth. You saw our breath between the gulps. I got silently stripped standing on the greenish socks it was so perishing. Lanna brought out the little black number, shoes and the stockings, then as I twisted and tugged the dress on, Lanna's hair touched my eyelashes while she leaned across tightening the bits on the suspenders. There was a tiny hole in the dress high up on the right shoulder above the basque. Lanna took a black felt-tip from her bag and, biting her lip, she coloured in my skin under the hole. I licked my fingers to roll the stockings up and lifted the dress while Lanna fixed the suspenders on. We put the long shirt, the velvet trousers, greenish socks and the baseball boots in the superstore bag. I put the steerhide jacket back on and checked the computer disc was still there. Arm in arm we walked over to The Mantrap.

The Slab, who was bouncer, put the carrier bag safe behind the counter where the downstairs of The Mantrap became a bakery during the day. On the first floor we stood in front of the mirrors in the toilet and Lanna tidied up my face and I used her lipstick that was any old colour.

In the big bar it didnt look like there were many seats. Everyone was there and mortal: Buttermountain, The Golden Binman, Overdose, Shadow, Tit, Pongo, Melon,

Sulee, The Shroud, J the Harbour, Goldfinger, Big Apple, Shagger, Superchicken, Lorne the Gas, Spook, The King Prawn, Cheese, whos called Suds since he started washing, Yellow Pages, The Dai Lama, Weed, Jimmy Gobhainn, that Four by Fours daughter, Marine Girl, The Seacow, a couple of the Dose brothers, that hippy girl Snowballs at the Moon, The Scoular, Synchro, Offshore, Smiler and Hailey.

Overdose was playing pool with two boys, one with the hair that I like; the boys werent port, maybe villages. When we squeezed by, Overdose says he was going to play them for his wife and he pointed to me. I smiled with Lanna but I turned beetroot.

Tequila Sheila waved. She was in a seat by the window and there was space, probably cause she was with The Panatine and Signal Passed at Danger. She was mortal on slammers as per usual. We slid along the seat and cause we couldnt afford anything, Lanna poured the last of the Southern Comfort into empty glasses. Tequila Sheila says His name but I just smiled and shrugged.

Tequila Sheila was telling Panatine the chef and SPD, who was a train driver with Red Hanna my fosterdad, about how she met her husband who was away in the jail: She was with two other girls watching three boys on the dancefloor so she had says, Yous two pick the ones yous want and I'll take the one whos left! We all laughed at this. You could hear the beat from up the stair. Though it was only bass and drums I could hear, you could tell it was that (Don't Fear) The Reaper, offof Some Enchanted

Evening. I used the goldish lighter on a Silk Cut after offering them round.

Lanna told about her last boyfriend, that one Saturday they used her parents' bed but he fell asleep drunk and wet it. Lanna had to dry the mattress by the window with a hair drier before her parents got back from work.

Thats nothing, says Tequila Sheila, who told how the summer she was housemaid in The Saint Columba she took this guy back to the staff flats while mortal on slammers and crashed out on him before anything could happen. She woke in the morning with him gone and this bouwfing smell so she sat up and was covered in it, cause he must have got down on his hunkers and done one right there on her stomach then put the toilet paper he used in her purse. Thats townies for you, Tequila Sheila says.

Thats nothing to what men will do, says Lanna, and told about Pheemy her pregnant sister who lives up the stair from them in The Complex. Lanna heard another argument so she ran up and let herself in. The brother-in-law had her sister's face in the scullery sink. He gave up and threw her on the lino shouting that if the dishes had been done like a decent wife should, the water would have been deep enough to drown her properly.

Tequila Sheila told about the first time she came to The Mantrap in high season, a boy asked her to dance and when she said No he pulled a flick-knife on her.

The two new faces walked by and Lanna bawls out about

them winning me. I smiled at the one with the hair that I like though they were both real honey-bunches.

Afraid not, says the blond. Central Belt accents. They were going up the stair to dance.

Theyll get their heads panned in, says Panatine.

Youve an admirer there Lanna, says SPD.

Naw, I think it's Morvern they fancy, Lanna says, then she told how she decided to do Tai Kwan Do lessons but when she phoned the number a voice had goes, Yes, can I take your order please? It was the Chinese carry-out who were doing it.

I just went hysterical at this and the others looked at me. Panatine laughed and asked if anyone wanted a wee goldie so I nodded.

Tequila Sheila was telling how she went to bed with a man the last summer. Afterwards he was going to put out the light. The man had took two totey-wee hearing aids out both ears. In the dark Tequila Sheila had went, Can you hear me? The man was silent.

We all were in hysterics at that then Panatine materialised with the whisky. I only drink whisky when I've a cold and chapped lips but I felt that sting then though I'd no chapped lip.

A good lot more ceilidhing went on and we were all mortal as newts. Lanna says, Hey, Morvern has a secret. My whole body jumped with fright.

Morvern's got a special knee. Come on, shows the boys your special knee cause it's Christmas, Lanna laughed.

It was only that so's I relaxed and reached up under the

little black number then undid the front eyehook on the left stocking. Panatine and SPD craned over. I lifted the leg to hold the knee under my chin then felt Lanna's fingers undo the back hook out of sight of the boys. Then Lanna licked her fingers and rolled the stocking down over my knee as I stretched the leg out. Lanna held the whole leg, bending it at the knee under the orangey lights from the ceiling.

See, see? goes Lanna.

Tequila Sheila sort of squeaked then groaned and says, Oh, aye, theres stuff glittering under the skin. SPD goes, Let's see let's see.

They could see the different coloured specks shining just under the surface of the skin and the whole knee sparkling when the beam of light caught it.

It's Christmas glitter, says Lanna.

Amazing, Panatine whispered.

These guys with tattoos across the way were really whistling at my bare thigh but Panatine and my group were just staring at the glistening knee.

It was when she was wee she came horsing in the scullery, slid on her knees and skinned one deep on these Christmas cards she was making and the glitter sunk right in her; they never got it all out her at The Hospital, says Lanna.

It was the first time I'd spoke that day if you dont count the swear-out-loud when my foot touched the blood that morning; cause I was mortal though I says: I can still remember. My fosterdad called 999 cause it was just gushing blood and by chance the ambulance was up The Complex. I got put in the back with a really young girl who was having a premature baby right there and then. The nurse told me just to watch all the way to the hospital to keep my mind off my cut knee. The girl was screaming and screaming and a wee baby girl was coming out.

There was no talking, then SPD says how the glitter would sink deeper and go invisible the older I got. Everyone was watching Lanna lick her fingers and roll the stocking back up my leg then me smiling and hooking the strap on the front and Lanna reaching behind.

I dont want the glitter to go away, I says, tugging down the dress.

Ah, but it will, Panatine went. There was a bit of no talking then Panatine asked if I got teased at school for having no known mother or father.

I told about a day in geography when we all had to do a talk about the village where we were born. When my turn came I'd goes that I didnt know what village I was born in so the whole class laughed and the teacher scolded me.

I told about how my fosterparents had says I was different from when I was wee but it was only before my fostermum died they explained I was orphaned.

I says how my fostermum couldnt have children so her and Red Hanna fostered me and took in other Special Girls every summer. I goes about the girl I shared the bunk with for summer. She always wore suppositories and changed them three times a day. Eventually she told me that her father used to attack her every night. She discovered that if she wore suppositories he couldnt get in her that way and I cuddled her all night.

Just then a fight broke out between the four men across from us. The one with the tattoos and another bawled, The Argylls, the two others, The Kosbys. Two climbed on one and brought him down on a table. Glasses broke and a man began pushing the neck of a beer bottle into another's eye, shouting how The Argylls was full of Fenians so he was going to get an eyeball in the bottom of the bottle to hold up to the light and see how green it was.

The Slab marched in, held something to his cigar and chucked it at the feet of the four fighting men. There was a big bang with screaming and smoke then the men holding their ears as The Slab charged in and two other barmen took pick handles to the legs of the fighters.

The Slab had thrown one of the big lifeboat fireworks he used. A guy passing says that you wouldnt believe the one with the tattoos had been on a life-support system since the last weekend.

I could hear Cameo going, so with all the Southern Comfort drunk Lanna and me bombed it up the stair to dance.

It was She's Mine offof the Wordup album and that went straight into Just Be Yourself that was only previously available on a twelve inch.

Lanna and me did little routines together with arms and legs in rhythm and we shook our hair lots. The boys who had been playing pool were there: the one with the hair.

Smiler was there, loafing about in his leather jacket with a pint. Lanna and me put our arms round him and kissed him on lips. We didnt say words just cheekily sipped from his pint then danced.

I knew all the music. I was trying to be ahead of the beat. My legs followed bass and drums while my arms and body were guitar or other noises. A whirling arm was a guitar solo. The boys moved over to us.

The boys bought Lanna and me beer in bottles and you could hold the bottles with two fingers while you danced, stopping on occasion to use the goldish lighter on a Silk Cut or Regal.

I danced with the one boy then the other and Lanna did too. There were Christmas songs.

The lights came up and you could see the sweat on Lanna's forehead.

You going home? Lanna says.

No ways, I goes.

The boys had a car and were going to a party so I got the steerhide jacket off a chairback and pulling it on I felt the disc in the pocket.

Lanna did my make-up in the toilets and all began moving into the night. As we filed out, Overdose was unconscious in the chair helping prop the door open. On the pavement people were shouting and hanging about. The King Prawn walked by with a massive carry-out of bottles in a bin-liner. A one-armed fisherman came up to Tequila Sheila. They went away together.

Everyone was watching The Lighthouse bar on the

north pier where the police had arrested so many they were using taxis to take them away.

Lanna and me walked arm in arm behind the boys. I was famished and they offered so we waited in the queue outside the baked-tattie shop. They always insist on putting meat in mine to fatten me up a bit so I had one with nothing on it; not even opened! Steam came whooshing out when I lopped the top off outside, using a comb from the guy with the hair and handing it back to him.

Lanna and me ate in the back and the car had a good stereo; REM doing Try Not To Breathe offof Automatic For The People. I was listening to the lyrics awful closely.

We were driving out the port, beside the sea towards the Back Settlement then below the fallen-down castle to the sands. Only well-to-do live there, in bought-houses.

Snow flakes began to fall. Lanna and me stuck our heads out the same window, biting the flakes and having hysterics till we mustve been blue in the face.

The party was in a big bungalow with an enormous brae for a garden. Inside I danced and banged the record player. I was given a can of Tennents. Some boy goes that his parents owned the house and they were away in a country. He turned and says to me about a university. How he designed houses there then what house I would want designed. All in his south accent. I says, One where you couldnt hear men go to the toilet. I was in stitches. The guy wouldnt dance so I did with Lanna and the boys. When Lanna and me talked to them we put our hands on their shoulders and shouted in their ears. They had the names John and Paul, like disciples.

People were chucking snowballs at the steamed-up windows and one pane of glass smashed. Me and Lanna ran out and chucked snowballs. The boy whose parents owned tried to stop it but there was a big snowball fight right through the house. A huge snowman was getting built in the modern scullery.

It snowed so thick it stuck to faces. Girls were using trays for sledges. Outside the Paul got me by the legs and tried to give me a fireman's lift. We fell and I couldnt get away for being in hysterics. He kissed me on the mouth and as he did it my mouth was the only warm bit I could feel. I skelpted him with snow down the neck. I remembered and my hand shot to the pocket but the computer disc was safe. There was a dead exciting running snowball fight with whole gangs screaming and laughing then I walked back up to the bungalow with the Paul.

In the scullery Lanna was kissing seriously with the John and people were putting a smiley face on the snowman using assorted veg from the cupboards. Lanna put her arm round me and goes how perished I was.

Two girls were gallivanting topless and Lanna whispered, Tarts. Some boys and girls from high school were having showers together and screaming cause others were throwing snowballs into the steamy bathroom. The boy who lived there had been tied up and locked in a cupboard where they found skis and the boy had gone fast asleep.

Some girls were skiing a slalom down the garden and smashing into the fence.

One of the topless girls walked right up to us and says, Theres another shower if yous are shy.

It was a wee shower room off a huge bedroom. The bed was covered in coats and jackets and a boy and girl sound asleep. There were dryish towels so Lanna and me go, in and locked the door. Everything came off and as per usual we got in together to save time. We tried not to get hair wet and soaped each other, laughing when she lathered the felt tip on my shoulder then the glittering knee. I washed in myself again that day and Lanna put her hand up on the tiles to wash right in her. Lanna says about wishing she was bigger in the chest and I goes that I had nothing to beat there and I was thin as a lat. We dried selves then dressed bumping each other in the little room.

Through the house a lot had gone and there was noise from one bedroom. Cans and bottles were everywhere and crisps or nuts crushed into carpets. There was broken glass under a window and the big smiling snowman in the scullery where some were still drinking.

The John and Paul had claimed a bedroom with electric fire, candles and some cans of Tennents. They had a pack of cards.

Let's play Strip Jack Naked, I blurted out.

We drank at the cans then eventually they got me down to the basque thing and one stocking but Lanna was topless with just the skirt and ankle chain. The males only lost shirts and socks. I was getting that bit rampant.

With a candle Lanna showed them my glittering knee and they both touched the skin with their fingers. Then she slowly lifted the basque from behind to show them the felt tip. Shadows were jumping on the ceiling and I felt sick. Lanna got me by the hand and took me into the bed. Night night and God bless, she says.

I woke. Getting offof the bed I stood on Lanna who was on the floor with both boys. In the toilet I locked the door and boaked three times.

I flushed the toilet and did my teeth with someone's brush. Through the scullery the floor was flooded with inches of water. I drank out a milk carton then started to greet. Lanna came from the bedroom with the steerhide jacket and put it round my shoulders. She started footering about, getting one stocking back on and straightening them; right enough they were in a proper kerfuffle. Lanna says, Come and watch *us*, as she left.

I sniffed. I felt the computer disc in the jacket pocket. I used the goldish lighter on a Silk Cut.

Oh Little Star of Bethlehem, offof Delay 68, was in my ears. I plucked up courage to take a keek in that room: In candlelight Lanna and the two disciples were bare on the bed doing everything. With her teeth together Lanna goes, It's *so* rampant. I watched a good while and a flush of rampantness went across me. I turned back to the scullery and sat alone. Waves of something kept going across till my face felt numb. There was freezing water at my stocking feet. The carrot that was the snowman's nose had fallen out. I touched the computer disc in the pocket and you just knew it had that message from Him on it.

It was only saliva I boaked up in the sink. I ran the tap. In the toilet I used the toothbrush twice. I helped myself to some talc, putting it here and there and that. Back in the scullery I took the milk carton out the fridge, had a swallow, then crossed the passage to that room, put the milk carton by the bedside and crawled in with the three nude bodies.

I let them do anything to me and tried to make each as satisfied as I could. I concentrated on the different positions. Later, cooried with my face near the window, all three of them were at my behind, and as the wave of something went across so strong I was smiling, I stared up and out. The dark sky above the port was empty of any little star.

ALL THE using of my mouth had kept the milk I drunk during the night from sticking round it. The Paul one dropped ash on the scullery table. You judge how many someone smokes by the neatness with ash. The Paul one was bumming his loaf about a university in a city and I should visit and that.

Lanna, the John one and girls with tops on were round a big pot mixing in different flavoured cans of soup.

I says, I'm just popping out for a wee breather. Outside I pulled up the smooth-running zip on the steerhide jacket then checked the computer disc. The bitter cold helped how poorly I felt.

There were lots of these little holes in the snow with footsteps leading up. I looked in one hole: frozen sick was at the bottom. It'd sunk when hot. A robin-red-breast was poking in another hole.

Lanna'd followed me out. I says, Your hair looks all lovely, ginger-nut. I'm going.

No cars can go on the roads. We'll get pneumonia in these clothes, Lanna says, her breath blowing sideways.

My toes were nipping before I'd turned the point by

the sea away from the bungalow. When I looked back Lanna'd gone back in. He Loved Him Madly was in my ears.

I walked with my teeth chattering, trying to plonk my feet down into the snow crust instead of forcing my ankles forwards breaking it up. The stockings got torn on the shins.

By the point under the fallen-down-castle I stepped from the road then looked at the sea and rocks where scuba divers go off in High Season. I stopped He Loved Him Madly in the ears.

The current moved by. At low tide you can go right round the rocks. My fosterdad took me when I was wee and I would look for the seabed to be of sand under water that was the colour blue, where I could go swimming like I'd seen in holiday brochures. We always went to the cold windy islands for our holidays with a Special Girl. I could never find a secret cove with beautiful sand under water that was the bright colour blue.

Just then a fishing boat came round the point, so close in I could see snow on the deck and the marks on the man's oilskin that was the orangey colour. I could have shouted easy. The man on the deck stared at me. I sumley supposed he thought I was bad luck or something cause a girl in black, like the dark water round his boat and the wet rocks where the saltiness had melted the snow. Quickly I lifted the little black number to show him the pale skin above the laddered stockings with the black lines of straps on my thighs. You felt the cold nip more. The boat moved into the bay till its engine was gone, the man still looking back as the wash melted snow off the rocks with a hiss. I covered myself up then used the goldish lighter on a Silk Cut.

I looked out to my fostermother's island where she lay buried. I got the day off for her funeral and wore my black school blazer. The relatives walked indian-file across the gangplank into the side of The Saint Columba. Drops of rain stuck to the deck windows of this thick glass with metal bolts round, then the drops moved in wind gusts as it got more daylight. I asked for tea and was given it with no milk or sugar then was too upset to say about its bitter taste.

You could feel engines through your feet, and at doors you stepped over a rim. The ferry moved backwards then forwards. It was queer seeing the port go sideyways through the wet glass. Red Hanna was fairly bolting the nips at the bar and telling how my auntie up from the south only wanted my fostermother's blueish brooch and what money there was.

At the farm, sheepdogs were wagging tails at all the people and the brothers drew lots for carrying the coffin. Up the stair the lid was off the coffin and she was lying with the primrose waistcoat on.

I was made to go up alone. All her savings were on the table in small piles of fivers with name tags by the piles. The blueish brooch was there with other bits of jewellery and more names on paper slips. Sure enough my auntie's name was written next to the brooch. The room stank of whisky fumes cause on another table were rows of different-shaped glasses with nips in. Before the hearse came, my fosterdad climbed up the stair alone, then he showed the undertaker up the stair to screw the lid on and the brothers carried the coffin out the front door.

My auntie up from the south was trying to be all hoity-toity, linking the other arm of Red Hanna when we followed the coffin out but Red Hanna says nothing. I sumley supposed she just couldnt wait to get back up the stair to the blueish brooch and the fivers. People who werent related were staying behind to make sandwiches.

In church the seats were hard and instead of coughs it was crying you heard in the silences. That graveyard was on a point near a hotel with sea all round. Clouds were flying along mountainsides above. The words of the Bible got blown away in the gusts. Red Hanna took me by the shoulders when I wouldnt leave. Gravediggers kept well away from us and the minute we left they got bent into that shovelling so's they could get out the rain.

Back at the farm my auntie from the south started screaming from up the stair straight away. Red Hanna had taken all my fostermother's money, jewellery and the blueish brooch then tucked them into the primrose waistcoat with her.

I was still stood there when Lanna come up to me with

her fingers spread and arms held out. I swept the jacket round her and gave her big bear hugs.

Huh, I'm petrified with the cold, she goes. Then she says, You missed the rich kid's soup.

We used the goldish lighter on Regals. With hands cupped round tips you could feel the glow when you inhaled.

Your stockings are ruined, I says kicking out my leg. Lanna just shrugged. Did you like them boys? I goes.

Nut, she shook her hair.

Neither?

Nut. Right townies.

We started crunching along past the fallen-down-castle in totally black clothes among all that whiteness. Our ankles sunk right down into deep bits. You knew we were going to start and when Lanna and me looked in each other's face we just went into the hysterics. You mustve been able to hear the laughs up where the first port houses start. You could probably hear them across the narrow Sound at the keeper's cottage by the point. We were in hysterics so much we couldnt walk straight and the snow didnt help. We walked a bit further on. There was a stuck car, all doors locked. Lanna says, Let's cut up to my Granny Couris Jean's for a bath and warm up. She's in the disabled houses and she's got the phone. We might get gumboots or coats. See, two year ago, before they moved her, she was in yon horrible top flat in Scalpy Crescent. The way her legs are she couldnt use the stairs, so when the rubbish got smelly she just chucked the bag

31

out the scullery window down the back green. She hates gulls so's she puts mustard on a heel-ender and chucks it out too. I used to wonder how Couris Jean got to her armchair, till one time I come in with the messages and found her crawling on the floor to the toilet.

In the port Couris Jean opened the door. She used a walking frame.

Youve been on the ran dan you couple of wee tinkers and your mother's up to high doe. Get by the bleezing fire then, yous must be perished the both of yous. Couple of wee monkeys. Been at a right hurrohrah-borealis. A right UpHellyAa, eh?

Granny, this is Morvern from the superstore.

Hello Granny Phimister, I says.

Get the whistlin jenny on, Couris Jean shouted.

By the fire we peeled our stockings right off and the blood came back into my fingers and toes. Lanna phoned her mum. You heard my name and whispers. Then I held a mug of tea in both hands and Lanna made buttered toast.

Couris Jean says, Away and get into a piping-hot bath the both of yous and the first one out gets the prettiest dress. She laughed like she was in hysterics as she got down in her armchair.

The bath had a rail for Couris Jean. There was a shower curtain but no shower. This was so's Couris Jean could pull it for a bit privacy when the home-help got her out

32

the bath. Me and Lanna sat in with our knees snug under each other's oxters.

What did you tell your mum? I says.

Just that we were over at yours and with the snow I thought I'd stay the night. After all you dont have the phone. Thats true enough, Lanna went.

We sat in the steam then Lanna shampooed my hair and I did hers at the same time, our arms reaching and stretching to lather up our heads. We mucked about with suds throwing them at each other. Scrubbed my knee. The felt tip and that.

I whispered, Everything was sort of doubled. It was the same way you kiss both lips when you just kiss a single mouth.

I know, I watched you, Lanna nodded to the bath water, They each tasted the same, eh?

Aye, I cant remember what one of them did what to me, y'know? I used nearly all the toilet paper in the morning.

Lanna laughed then quickly says, What are you going to tell Him about last night then? Anything?

Lanna He's gone.

Eh? she goes.

He's gone. Thats why I had presents early.

A look came on her face and she went, How do you mean He's gone?

Gone. He's not with me now.

Well gone where? she says.

You know He's lived in countries.

She sat down in the empty tub and went, He's gone to

33

a country? But yon stuff he puts on His computer and the model train set?

He's not coming back.

When did He go then? Her mouth was by my middle and you could feel her breath on me.

Yesterday.

I'll get some more towels, Lanna says.

We sat by the red hot coals drinking cocoa. We had towels round us and on our heads. I was starting the nodding off then the Meals On Wheels arrived for Couris Jean. The woman driver told about how she couldnt get to some houses and how some old folk couldnt afford heating. The big metal soup urn was in the open air and some snow was stuck to the bottom of it, as if poor people were in a war that no one else was.

Still in towels we did Couris Jean's dishes then Lanna showed the spare room and says, Have a little lie down.

I put on the basque and knickies then goes, Wont you come?

Later, she says watching me.

When dozing, old hands come under the downie and put a hot water bottle in. You could hear the walking frame creak. I held the bottle to the basque and through the bag of water you could hear my heart going. It was the first time I'd slept alone in four year and you only listen to your heart when you sleep alone. I had kept my wrist watch on cause there was no one to scratch.

I woke and felt queerish. I could tell it was nighttime by the type of voice on telly. I was pouring sweat. I wiped my forehead with the back of my arm then pulled on the little black number. I straightened the bed then poured the water from the bottle down the scullery sink.

In the room only the moving light from telly lit Couris Jean, sitting up straight. Lanna wasnt there. The stee. hide jacket hung on a seat.

Couris Jean says, Allanah is way up The Complex in gumboots. I've another leaky pair. You were away in the land of nod so's we didnt want to wake you.

I checked the computer disc then took out the goldish lighter and a Silk Cut.

Are you perished pet? Come away and sit next to the fire here. Put a bit more coal on if you want to help me, she says.

I sat at her feet on the hearth and smiled up then I plonked on two more lumps and wiped my fingers on the little black number.

I've a coat for you too, she says.

Is it all right to smoke? I went.

Oh aye. I'm not fussy.

I used the goldish lighter on the Silk Cut. I says, Would you fancy some tea Granny Phimister?

I infused the two mugs and sat back on the hearth

running my hands over the bristles coming on my legs. I used the goldish lighter on another Silk Cut. I was about to show her the glittering knee.

So youre the Callar girl. Youre very quiet Morvern, for a friend of Allanah's.

I'm no really when you get to know me.

We both laughed. I says, Aye Lanna and that at the superstore think I'm a right queer-case for not talking. I'm taciturn.

Whats that?

It's a word my boyfriend told me. It means you dont really say much.

Oh it's a word is it?

Aye. There was a long bit of silentness except telly.

Whats this man of yours like?

I says, He grew up in the village at the far end of the pass, just beyond the power station. His father owned that hotel at the top of the stairs above the railway there, that hotel with the pointing-up tower below the Tree Church.

The Tree Church, I remember yon, says Couris Jean.

Aye, the gardeners in the big house cultivated it over the years; grew it and shaped it. Evergreen hedge for the walls with arch-shaped holes cut in for windows. The gardeners have trimmed a big roof-shape and in the summertimes the door has a rose bower round. Theres a few benches inside and a thing for the holy water.

Couris Jean goes, Used to be that in the summertimes, couples from that village could get married inside and babes christened if they got permission from the big house.

I says, Well He grew up in the hotel below the little Tree Church. His father sold the hotel then they retired away to a country and He left as well and lived in countries. Some years back he suddenly appeared off the train; the 12.55.

When I stopped there was no talking. I sniffed and took a swallow tea.

So yous live together then?

We rent a top flat and loft in Burnbank Terrace.

How long have you been going?

Five year, since I was sixteen. One day he came in the superstore, walked up to the till with the biggest box of chocolates they sell then strolls back across the floor to where I'm working at the produce section and just hands the box to me in front of everyone's eyes, I laughed.

Couris Jean smiled, What age will he be now?

He's thirty-four. Queerest of all is the model railway-set of his childhood village he's built up in the loft. He's such a contrary so-and-so, not really a one for toy trains you'd suppose but there it is. He's spent hundreds till it seems exactly like the real thing, so he sits up there just doing these big stares at it; from the railway line to the top of the stairs and the hotel with the pointing-up tower, to the graveyard path above where you see an exact little model of the actual Tree Church all flowered in a summer-time. Then you see the pylons stood up along the sides

37

of the pass, up towards the dam of the power station. I've got all that right up there in my loft.

Does he not work?

He seems to have a bit money hidden away. He has this computer and god alone knows what He's always putting in to that, He doesnt let me see; He's always saying He doesnt have much time.

How does Mr Callar take to him?

There were rows and ructions at home when I was sixteen but they know he's good to me.

He's good to you then?

Aye.

He should have the gumption to; you look like an angel come to this earth, says Couris Jean.

I used the goldish lighter on another Silk Cut and says, Do you know my fosterdad then?

No as well as some of the other Callars way back when. They were from the same island as your fostermummy.

Aye? I thought it was a mainland name?

No, no. You dont know the story about your own name? They say when yon galleon went down off the island your fosterdaddy's people were descendants of them, says Couris Jean.

What, in fifteen-something?

Aye. Thought we were all cannibals. They sat out in their big sailing boat and were too feart to come ashore so they floated in a row boat full of live hens. The locals were waiting to welcome them on the sands but when the boat was pulled out the water they just found hens on it.

The locals mustve thought they were all a bit touched, wonky in the head, you know? So they left them anchored out there but a right gale blew up and the galleon turned turtle. The ones who never drowned were up on the beach in the morning. They couldnt speak a word of Gaelic but they mustve got by the same way I did cause they married local girls and your fosterdad's name is said to come from that.

How d'you mean, the same way you did? I went.

Couris Jean says, I never spoke for four year, till I was your age. When I married my husband he'd never heard my voice. I was sixteen in that heatwave it was. My family had the tenant croft at the sea there before the Back Settlement. A' Phàirce Mhóir, The Big Park, that croft was called. My father and mother would all go away with my three brothers, droving to the mart here in port. In those days it was quite usual to leave me with just the dogs, alone.

That was such a heatwave at midnight I could read the penny dreadfuls outside when I woke up, swung out of my bed and dandered down onto the sand at the water's edge. The sea was smooth right out. I was in my birthday suit and no person was going to be around at that unearthly hour. It was lovely to feel the puffs of breeze right there on places it'd never been. I stood with my arms folded on my paps, like this. I was getting a real feeling in my tummy, all awful alive, but the dogs started to howl up behind the gate, then out the water in front of me in that bluey light, up rose the great white horse moving its head from side to side as it came over the sand towards me and more horses came bursting out the water, rearing up onto the beach, a dozen horses, two dozen horses running in front of me and splashing drops of salty water on my face while two score more horses came out the sea, running in front of me and running behind me. I sat down on my bahookie, the sand shuddered from all the hoofs galloping, and as the ground shook I got this feeling so strong for the first time ever, then I just put my eyes down on my knees and covered my ears.

I was cooried there like that in the morning, the horses gone, with my staring brothers round me so one put his big jacket over my shoulders to cover everything.

They tried to explain how a cargo boat carrying horses for the war had capsized way out in the Sound and the horses that hadnt gone down swam ashore, just happening on my beach, but I didnt breathe another word for four years after that night.

I whispered, You went silent?

It was the fright. Then I spoke my husband's name on our wedding night and when we had Allanah's father I started talking to the baby, Gaelic then a bit English.

She gave me gumboots and her old overcoat. The lapels on the coat were stained pinkish with rouge from the days when Couris Jean could make it to The Politician bar. I had on the gumboots and put the stained coat on top the steerhide jacket. The shoes Lanna'd lent were put in the

bag with the superstore name written off it. I hugged
Couris Jean. While I walked up The Complex I was sweating under the old coat.

What on earth are you wearing? Red Hanna my fosterdad
says.

I walked into the council flat I'd grown up in. Red
Hanna had been watching the same telly programme as
Couris Jean.

I'm ill.

Whats wrong? Wheres He?

Gone, I says. My face was all slidey with sweat. I
pushed the door to my old bedroom. It was cold and the
curtains werent pulled. I stripped off and looked under
the bed: the big coiled escape rope that Red Hanna kept
in case of fire was still there. Wearing the basque I got
under the sheet on the bottom bunk. I started shaking.
Red Hanna put the bar fire in the room, pulled the curtains
then left, shutting the door.

My fosterdad was on a scullery chair pulled next to the
bed and he was pushing hair away from my eyes. He
says, She's coming soon.

I'll be nice to her, I goes.

He laughed then brought barley water in a tumbler and
tucked the tartany rug in under the sheet.

Will I put the light out? Red Hanna says.

I nodded the once.

I heard voices in my doze. Someone came in the dark to look at me. I opened my eyes. You could see Vanessa the Depresser's hair all sticking up. I shut eyes.

I dreamed all the time, tossing and turning. When I got up it was to cross to the toilet and run both taps to cover the noise of me having the skitters.

On Christmas morning you could smell food. Grey-looking snow was blocking a bit of the window. Sometimes you heard laughing.

Bare, sitting on a beach with bluey sea so lovely like in brochures, the horse heads came out the water but fixed to men bodies. All the bare bodies had a hand missing. The menhorses walked up and surrounded me. Blood came from the missing hands when they turned me over to attack. I saw Lanna and a fisherman out in a rowing boat, watching closely.

My body jerked awake and it was dead of night. The sheet was all fankled. My nose was stuffed up and my throat was sore. It hurt to turn my head. I was going to boak: I made the window and opened it but most of the sickness hit the window-sill in a heap. I breathed in cold air and looked out across The Complex all covered in snow with moonlight on it. The Complex where I'd had to grow up. Where one young husband owned a camcorder so his four married brothers and him swapped porno videos of their unknowing wives.

On boxing day, V the D, who was primary school teacher from the Back Settlement and Red Hanna's ladyfriend, come in with a tray of tea and porridge.

Sorry for ruining Christmas here, I've split with my boyfriend and he's left, I says.

Dont exaggerate, goes V the D.

Dont open those curtains, I went.

She did and screamed.

Merry Christmas, I says.

I woke and Red Hanna was on the scullery chair. He lit two Regals and handed me one. He nodded, smiling at the window. I smiled back.

I've brought your presents, he says and put a big shiny packet on the bed. Inside was a short orangey-coloured summer dress and dear-looking mirrored sunglasses from V the D.

Oh, thanks, I goes.

For the summer if it comes. We were kind of hoping

you'd come over to the islands with us this year, says Red Hanna.

I was sort of saving for a resort. I was going to ask Lanna to come but she's skint and it'll be a fight to get our holidays together, I goes.

Well. Whatever, Red Hanna says. There was a long bit of silentness. Red Hanna goes, I thought He was a good thing but evidently not. Where will you live?

I'll keep up that place, maybe get Lanna in on yon pull-down couch. She wants to get out The Complex after all.

Gone for good?

Aye, I goes.

Well He's a fool. Has He run out of money or something?

He's left all His stuff: the model railway, the computer and all those books. I can sell it. He's away to a country.

Ah, Morvern. All the love in the world rising up leaving just hate.

Theres still small pleasures though, I says.

But no big pleasures for the likes of us, eh? We who eat from the plate thats largely empty. I've saved for this early number, now it's coming I feel empty, the overtime has just gobbled up the years and heres you, twenty-one, a forty-hour week on slave wages for the rest of your life; even with the fortnight in a resort theres no much room for poetry there, eh?

Are you going out to the Back Settlement with her then?

Aye. I'm happy with her Morvern, the four months to

44

run and I'll get my lump sum. Its a lovely bungalow. Loads to do in her garden. That view of Beinn Mheadhonach and the Pass from the window as night comes on. Red Hanna lit two more Regals then says, The hidden fact of our world is that theres no point in having desire unless youve money. Every desire is transformed into sour dreams. You get told if you work hard you get money but most work hard and end up with nothing. I wouldnt mind if it was shown as the lottery it is but oh no. The law as brute force has to be worshipped as virtue. Theres no freedom, no liberty; theres just money. Thats the world we've made and no one tells me to find more to life when I've no time or money to live it. We live off each other's necessities and fancy names for barefaced robbery. Yet what good is all the money in the world to me now when all I want to do is stare out the bungalow window at the mountains? Money would destroy what I've learned to accept over the years. In plain language, I'm fifty-five: a wasted life.

Red Hanna stood up and left but he was back with a glass of whisky, swirly with water. He was well glazed. He went, I had a friend saving for the rainy day. Just like me he had about six months to retirement. The Stick, a drummer in the ceilidh bands. Sixty-four years of age. There were no early retirement schemes in them days way before we adopted you. I was a fireman then, steam engine days. We were shoving back empty fish wagons on the pier sidings. Before the tracks were lifted. So's we come up against the wagons and The Stick never emerged from between them, you know? So's I climbed down off the engine, walks along there and The Stick was crushed, still alive and totally conscious, between two buffers but with his rib cage squashed up like this, about six inches left between these buffers. So along come the fire brigade and the doctor; cut away the boiler suit offof his arm and give him a jag. Fire brigade told that they couldnt free him. We couldnt use the engine to separate the wagons cause one back-movement would close up the few inches between the buffers and squeeze the life out him. My driver was Barra and he was in tears but he wouldnt let anyone else ease the engine and two top wagons away so gently, leaving The Stick trapped between the other two wagons. I says to The Stick that everyone was going to tug the wagon offof him with a rope then they'd rush him up to the hospital. He just whispered, could he have a smoke. I started making this roll-up but the manager went, For christsake, and hands The Stick a cigarette from his silver case. I lit it and placed it in The Stick's lips, holding it and taking the cigarette out for each wee puff he managed. All the men gathered round, watching silently. I remember that the butt was stained pink offof his lips. Well at long last that cigarette was gone and The Stick just whispers, Right, pull it away. The fire brigade had a rope on the hook of the top wagon and all us men, must have been forty of us: railway, fishermen, piermen, fellows from the ice factory; we all grabbed that rope and with one tug the wagon pulled forward smoothly behind us and it was clamped quick. The Stick stood straight up, took one step forward, was stock still then suddenly all these black guts pushed out his mouth, his legs wobbled and he fell on the rails dead.

I dozed a while then I got up. In the bathroom I used Red Hanna's razors and shaving foam on my legs. On top of the spray can the words for Good Morning were round the rim in all different languages.

I had a shower then helped myself to plenty of V the D's talc and moisturiser, putting it here and there. I got into the new short summer dress not bothering with the basque or anything on my feet.

Hi, I goes to her.

Tomorrow off too? she says.

I nodded, heating some left-over soup and roast tatties.

There were no good films on telly and Red Hanna was so mortal V the D had to put him to bed. Lanna phoned me up and asked if she could come round with my presents but I says to leave it till work cause I'd another wee thing for her. I goes about Couris Jean's stuff and I'd get Red Hanna to drop it off. She says, You sound all choked up with the cold.

I'm pretty jiggered, I goes.

Oh, pet, Lanna went.

After V the D dawdled off to bed I looked at the changing lights coming from the telly and showing across the room.

I used the goldish lighter on Silk Cuts then put my head in my hands for a good bit. I curled my bare legs on the couch then after a while I got up to turn off telly. I sat in the light coming from the heater and showing across the room. At some time I pulled the short dress up.

You couldnt remember what one, but one had taken my right bosom and Lanna's left bosom, then ever so careful placed the points together so both our hard nipples were rubbing then he gently took both in his mouth, sucking and licking them together in such a surprising and loving way with Lanna looking me in the face all the while he did it.

I let my hair touch the floor just as I made it happen, remembering. I wiped my finger high up on the curve of my bottom and pulled the short dress down. After a bit I put the heater out and toddled off to the bunk.

It was just sheeting rain in the night, clearing the roads a bit, but snow was all on the hill above The Complex. Red Hanna was backshift, going out on the twenty to six train, so I did a boiled veg with cheesy sauce. V the D gave us a lift down the road and they were going to drop off the gumboots and coat at Couris Jean's on the way to the station. Tell her, thanks, I says. When we parked outside my flat I told Red Hanna I'd leave their presents at the station. I'd ask yous up for coffee sometime but I've loads of clearing out to do, I says. V the D crunched the clutch and didnt use her mirror pulling out.

In the flat I got a new pack from the carton and used the goldish lighter on a Silk Cut. I put Secondhand Daylight by Magazine on the record player. I switched on and put the needle to Rhythm of Cruelty, the second track on Side One. Then I took out the live album Play and just put all Side One on. I set the Christmas tree on very fast then plugged in the heater. I took the computer disc out the steerhide jacket and looked at it. I opened the desk drawer. His Autocard for the hole-in-the-wall was there. I took out the Autocard, tossed in the disc and shut the drawer. Through in the bedroom I piled the dirty sheets in the corner and made the bed. I changed sides on the record. Dead on the scullery floor, He wasnt even smelly.

Next morning was payday. It was still raining and I got my period. I was up at sixish. I collected my bag from the downstair bakery under The Mantrap then in the Staff Only bothy at the station I dropped off Red Hanna and V the D's presents. Coll and SPD were there. About to go out on the twenty to eight, SPD says, hows the magic knee? I just laughed.

At the work all was as per usual. I got to sort the load. I gave Lanna her presents: that locket she wanted and my old leather jacket she always loved. I says, Sorry it's not much. She gave me a big bear hug and from her I got the video of Miss .45 The Angel Of Vengeance. I'd been trying to order it for ages and she'd had to post away for it. Also I got a dead brilliant dear-looking pedicure set. Look, I says, we'll have a video party at Hogmanay. Lanna goes if I'd heard from Him. I went, No.

After the work Bill Nelson's Red Noise was in the ears as I walked home. On principle I never shopped at the superstore and I turned carrier bags inside out. Up at the freezer shop I bought easy-cook pizza cause of the body on my scullery floor.

Back in the flat I chucked away the bit mail from model shops in the south. Trying to get in the oven to heat the pizza His body caused the usual hassles but I soon had it underway.

Watching telly while eating you only saw men machine-gunning in a ruined town. It was Yugoslavia then there was a picture of a girl human with the head missing. I put off the channel and watched the video of Bad Lieutenant while trying the bits of the pedicure set. I finished off using some Dusky Cherry on my toenails; my toes all splayed by the toe-dividers stuffed in between.

When Bad Lieutenant finished I did a big breath on account of the sadness of it. I put Iron Path by Last Exit on the record player turned up to 8. With the loft hook I tugged down the hatch. I stretched and pulled the end of the ladder down to the floorboards then I climbed up into the darkness. It was cold up there. There was no bulb in the rafter fitting. I pressed:

POWER

The hum of the transformer came and I switched on Nighttimeness.

Nighttimeness was in the little village beyond the power station at the far end of the pass. Tiny lights showed here and there. You saw the railway line and at the top of the stairs the hotel with the pointing-up tower, the graveyard path above and the tiny Tree Church flowered as per usual cause of the always summerness of the model village. I shoved in the switch. The humming stopped and there was dark except from the two skylights up in the rafters, moonlight was showing in two rectangles across the baby house slates of the village. Milky light on the mountainside where the pylons came down made it real.

I climbed down the ladder then fetched the new mirrored shades from the bedroom. I pulled on the scullery gloves then grabbed a leg. The leg moved then the whole body jerked in a movement that frightened you. I dropped the leg: it didnt move like a living thing at all. I did a big breath and my heart was racing. I stretched my fingers in the tight plastic gloves, bent down and gave a good tug. He was heavier than a six-wheeler loaded with tatties. I got Him under the ladder leaving a long smear down the corridor. The new mirrored shades had come in handy cause the blood wasnt so bright reddy as it came fresh from under His body.

Up in the loft I got the end of the spare pulley rope and hauled it back down the ladder with the ratchet clicking away. I tied the rope round His ankles then climbed back up into the loft where I put the shiny ratchet handle in the winch like He showed me when I helped Him build the model of His childhood village. I began turning the handle the other way and wound Him up the ladder towards me. His mouth hit every rung on the way up and I thought His hand was going to come off but it was quite sturdy and was still attached on. He swung into the loft when His face cleared the hatch and His bottom came near me then twisted away.

I had to go down the ladder to change sides on the record and I used the goldish lighter on a Silk Cut while knocking off from the job for a bit.

Back up the ladder I tied His arms to the other pulley rope then wound the body up till it was hanging, spinning a little, over the baseboard of the huge model. I turned the other ratchet then released the brake: the body crashed down onto the buildings of His childhood village smashing in one side of the mountain then lying still, face up to the skylights.

His toes at the far end of the pass. His face beyond the

railway line. His body crushed the hotel with its pointing-up tower at the top of the stairs. The Tree Church on the sgnurr above where he lay back upon the land.

I opened both skylights with the hook. Two rectangles of moonlight were on His bare body. I climbed down leaving the hatch open. I put on some of my own music rather than His: Spiral Tribe Sound System Sirius 23 and a tape of some DJs, that bootleg of The Mutoid Waste Company too.

I scrubbed the blood off the floor, drawing a tissue over the boards till no grime showed. I chopped the stained rug in bits then I washed the cleaver and knife and hung them back up above the sink. You could see He'd taken a good chunk out the table when the cleaver had come down on the hand. I wound the video of The Passenger forward to the bit where his wife is watching the news film of the firing squad on a beach. You could tell it was actual. After they shot, the nerves or something made the slouched man's face slowly look up. I rewound that bit then watched the whole film to its sad end.

I put one of His records on called Stravinsky Ballets (Orpheus side) then climbed up the ladder.

It'd started snowing again and flakes spun in through the skylights to the music. His lips were dusted with a layer falling right onto them.

I untied the ankle knot then re-rigged the main pulley. As I wound the handle, the model on its baseboard rose smoothly up, taking the weight of His body nearer the skylights, then it stopped under the rafter, snow flakes twirling down on the summer land, coating the sides of the pass, layering the village roofs and the giant man, layering the flowered roof of the Tree Church above Him. Some moonlight came through the skylights with the soft fall and it shone on the snow.

THERE WAS a real thunderplump. The rain was just coming down in sheets so's the water was dripping over my ears and you couldnt use the Walkman. Wipers of all cars and lorries made that noise and hands wiped from inside at the steamy windscreens leaving those finger shapes.

At the cash dispenser I stared at greenish numbers, His balance:

£6,839

You'd never have dreamed of so much money being yours, never in a month of Sundays. I withdrew the daily limit. He used to get me to withdraw on His card for telly, video, electric and rent. I put the Autocard back in my purse. With that kind of money there were cassettes you could get from the mail list and you could send away for bobby-dazzler clothes out the catalogue and get extra driving lessons on top the ones He'd already paid for. I walked straight to the travel agent.

Under the leaky station roof I shook out my hair and used the goldish lighter on a Silk Cut, nodding to the occasional person who was railway.

The L-car gave way then filtered into the station square with Ramraider next to yon blonde from the bank. She'd been gormless enough to wear a dress that Ramraider looked down as she turned round doing the reversing in. You always wore baggy jumpers and jeans for a lesson from The Ramraider but he still licked his lips when you climbed in and put on the seat belt. The Ramraider was no blether though, he only told about The Highway Code. The driving lessons happened mostly in a sensible silence then me answering Highway Code at the end: they were restful. I threw the butt in a puddle.

Wipers on in first, I started the lesson, revving a bit high in second to get behind the Alginate backshift bus. Beyond the north pier I got up into fourth and did forty then changed down smoothly at the filter by the Gathering Halls. I followed traffic down the Golden Mile glancing at the lucky so and so's doing a left and taking the way up the steepness then away from the port on the open roads.

I slowed for the only traffic lights, beyond St John's Square then round past the Christmas tree and the superstore where I had to work after the lesson. Up at the start of the glen you practise three-point-turns outside the golf clubhouse.

On the way back Ramraider hit the dash and I did a good emergency stop, pressing my foot down till you thought the wheels would lock then taking the squeeze off and re-applying till we stopped. The Ramraider nodded and smiled. So did I.

The high school to the Give Way, indicate right at The Mantrap, left at The Kale Onion. Hill-start below the stone folly, down Burnbank Terrace where the flat is, my windows below those skylights where His body lay. The telephone box, the Phoenix, the Bayview, along the seawall to the parking under the station clock where someone else was waiting for their lesson. Ramraider was in no hurry though and asked a good few Highway Code questions. He always asked a motorway question though there are no motorways near the port for a hundred miles.

My favourite bit of the questions was the road signs and I never got them wrong cause some nights I sat in bed with The Highway Code, remembering them. The sign I love most is Quayside or Riverbank:

Work was as per usual. Lanna told us Shadow the shelf-stacker pinched the Sexual Harassment video from Creeping Jesus's office and was using it at home with his wee brother cause the touching-up scene made him so rampant.

On Hogmanay I was early at The Kale Onion Hotel. It's really called The Caledonian Hotel, but the 'D' fell off the big sign and they never ever bothered to fix it.

I handed over a twenty after ordering a half pint cider and lager mixed with a shot Pernod then frothed up with blackcurrant. I used the coins from the change for the cigarette machine then as per usual I put 117/142/039 on the juke box. I balanced the half pint of frothy, purplish drink on top the screen then used the silver on Formula One. I was first in three races then third in the last so I still got onto the next level. When I hit an oil patch and came fifth in the race, I popped the coins into the collection box making the little lifeboat come out the shed and down the slip, then I sat for a good while at an empty table, tapping Silk Cut ash into the ashtray.

When new folk breezed in the door through Silk Cut and Embassy smoke you saw their mouths move straight away to the lyrics of the songs even before they spoke the words of their orders over the bar.

The Hiphearan came in carrying a plastic bag with the superstore name written off it. The Hiphearan's only way of getting money, apart from signing on, was leaping off the railway pier in High Season wearing his tackity boots, if the young holiday makers would pay him a fiver. He was quite an attraction and you would see him standing at some bar in the port with a big puddle round his feet. There was a photo of the Hiphearan in The Lighthouse bar. He was in the water trying to put his arm round a seal.

The Commander came in and saluted. He was one of the fastest Christmas posties but he wasnt getting to do it any more. When they started demolishing those condemned flats in Scourie Street they found four year of

Christmas mail stacked up behind one door. He sat beside The Hiphearan.

Red Hanna came in with Coll and SPD in tow. Red Hanna shouted, How was the lesson?

I sort of pushed my lips out and nodded.

Whats your pleasure? my fosterdad goes. I just shook my head and pointed to the drink in front me. That lot started a carry on, each trying to buy the round first. When they came over, Coll nodded to the Glory Hole beside the 777 machine, Whats that brain fever juice youre drinking Morvern? he says. Come away in the bothy here with us learned gentlemen, or are we all too old for you? Coll took a magic marker and Sellotape from his jacket and started making the wee sign that he stuck on the fruit machine so's young folk wouldnt bother him:

OUT OF ORDER

I sat down with them, listening to their blethering. Last year's football was on and the instant the adverts started all men's heads turned away from the telly at the same time and they started talking.

Lanna swanned in with the Bakery Girls. When I gave her a hug I goes in her ear, Let me get yous a drink, I'm deep pocketed so just sponge offof me all night, dont get into a rounds thing.

When I brought back the rounds Red Hanna was telling about The Commander who'd been next to me while I was getting served. The Bakery Girls kept going into hysterics. Red Hanna says, On Christmas Eve the police found him down on the shore by the north pier. He was flashing a torch out into the Sound and when the sergeant asks what he's doing, The Commander went and goes that he was signalling to enemy submarines to try and confuse them. All round the table burst out laughing and some looked over at the poor old soul.

The Panatine breenged in and over to the bar. He had his right hand circled in dirty bandage and the pinkie was just a blob of cotton wool; he was spilling the pint in his left hand that always twitched anyway from the time he sliced a nerve in his arm when he was the butcher. He stood in the Glory Hole shaking a bit and says, See this port, I love it, I just love it, best crack on earth. I could never leave here or I'd just burn up on re-entry. That was some session folks, some session. He took a big swallow of his pint then goes, I've just discharged myself from the hospital, they were trying to keep me in. Hogmanay up in the old sanatorium? No chance.

Look at the state of you man, went SPD.

The Panatine gulped back more lager then says, See that taxi driver, The Skiabhanach or whatever he's called, that guy is claimed. I'm going to jump on the guy's chest and gallop right through his guts.

Whats up? Lanna went.

The guy's guilty of mutilation. Human torture, man! Night before last I got yon trawlerman, Mockit, the one who always misses his sailing and has to race round the country trying to catch it at the next port, no mind the guy?

Oh aye, that berserker, he's some space cadet, says SPD.

More like a Starship Captain, goes Panatine. Then he says, Anyway, for a crack me and Mockit injected whisky into each other's temples, Macallan twelve-year-old of course. I love the subtle smokiness of the Macallan. We were steaming out the mind totally mortal within ten seconds. I scratched Mockit all over his face with the hypodermic trying to scoosh that malt right in his brain box. After that we put liquid LSD onto our pupils using the eyedropper. It enters the blood stream through your eyes and theres these amazing visual and retinal images. We could only see colours till five in the morning and by that time I was thinking about getting a few beers. The singular place I could think of to get a drink was on the ferry so I came down here and bought four return tickets to the island; one for every sailing. I went back and forth all day till the captain had me carried down the gangplank. By the time I found The Complex I'd lost my keys and I couldnt remember the wife's name, swear to christ it'd gone clean out my head so I just started battering in the front door. The wife thought it was Strathclyde's Finest busting us again so buckets of hot water were coming down from the bathroom window. I took a runner and the door smashed right in, came swinging back, and all I felt was it konking me in the face but I woke up in the hospital, just the-now. What happened was the wife had come down the stair and jets of blood were sprayed all up the wallpaper in the hall and I was out-the-game on the doormat so she runs and actually calls Strathclyde's Finest thinking I've been stabbed cause there's so much blood. The house is just dripping with heesh as well and the pigs arrive with an ambulance. They cart me straight off and twenty minutes later the phone goes in the house. The wife picks it up and it's the surgeon from the hospital, asking politely if she can perhaps find my pinkie by the door and sure enough: there it is down the side of the mat. The door had swung back and severed it when I elbowed my way in. Now the surgeon, he expresses the urgency that exists in the wife getting round to the hospital with my elusive digit so it can be sewn back on. So what does she do? Skins up and phones a taxi then when it arrives she pops my pinkie in an empty packet of crisps. Now this Skiabhanach is driving the taxi and can you believe this? He starts haggling over the taxi fare to the hospital! Stuff about it being against hygiene laws. My wife explains it's a Mercy Mission. So eventually he chucks the crisp packet in the glove compartment and drives off. Thing is on the way over to the hospital he was seen by reliable witnesses picking up a fare over to the Back Settlement. Took three quarters an hour to get the finger to the operating theatre and it was too late to sew it on. Then Strathclyde's Finest came back to the house when they knew I was comatose in hospital, bust the wife and took away all the plants.

You must be devastated, says Coll.

What, about the plants? goes Panatine.

No man, about your finger.

The Panatine held up both hands with the fingers spread out and shouted, One down; nine to go! He took two big gulps and drained his pint.

Just one thing, Red Hanna says, What flavour was the crisp packet? Everyone started laughing at this, especially Panatine waving the bandaged hand about.

Coll says, See me the other night. I come in the house full as a whelk and hung my overcoat on the post at the banister-bottom with my cap on the top. I was *so* crammonded I had to get on my knees to do the toilet. When I came out the bathroom what I saw was this guy in an overcoat and cap at the bottom of the stairs. I shouted, Who the hell are you and what're you doing in my house, then gave a left jab skinning all my knuckles on the wood, see?

Everyone chuckled at this but not with the same energy they'd put into laughing at the goings-on of The Panatine.

Lanna gave me a signal so we went in the toilets. A sign written in magic marker was Sellotaped to the Tampax machine:

OUT OF ORDER: AVAILABLE AT BAR.

Lanna opened her packet of Regal. Inside were five cigarettes and two rolled joints.

Where'd you get them? I says.

Oh round here-ish. Fancy?

No, I'll just get bad dreams, I goes.

63

Eh? Look as well, went Lanna opening her purse. There were two tabs.

Ah, no thanks Lanna.

Whats the matter with you? It's those videos you watch that give you the dreams. Oh well, stick, she says and swallowed one of the tabs then climbed up on the toilet in the cubicle. I followed her in and sat on the toilet-edge while she smoked the joint, blowing out the window.

Are you still coming back to watch the videos? I says.

Aye, I says I would didnt I?

Thought you might want to go first-footing.

Nut. Who are you going to Hog-snog when the bells go? says Lanna.

I havent thought about it, I goes.

Lanna climbed down and took out a card in an envelope from her shoulder bag. The John and the Paul's second names and some address in The Central Belt were written on the envelope with a stamp on it.

Where did you get their address? I says.

They gave it me. I thought we should just send a card, here you write it. Lanna handed me the black felt tip.

I mused for a few secs then wrote:

CHEERS FOR BUMPIN US

MORVY & LANNA

X X X X X X X

Lanna laughed then sealed up the envelope. I handed her the felt tip and she started writing graffiti on the locked toilet door:

Get lost, I says and grabbed the felt tip off her. I bit the end a while then wrote:

LANNA PHIMISTER SAYS — SASSY SINGLE BAKERS ENJOY
IT BETTER FROM BEHIND.

We both laughed. Then suddenly we heard the bells going and some fishing boats hooting out by the pier. Lanna screamed and dropped what was left of her joint into the toilet. Lead the way, she goes.

We bombed through and I got kissed by a few grey heads. Lanna started kissing everyone. The Commander, The Hiphearan, SPD, the Bakery Girls, Coll, The Panatine, one-legged Cushion and I watched her and Red Hanna cuddle.

Happy new year Morvern, Red Hanna goes and kissed me on the cheek. He says, Hope it's a prosperous year for you beautiful. I nodded and sat down. All were mortal, shaking hands and snogging and knocking back drinks. Some folk were moving off to go first-footing but there were fresh rounds on our table so I started drinking and using the goldish lighter on Silk Cuts.

Lanna was sat next to The Panatine who was saying to one-legged Cushion, Remember thon night I gave you a tab before you came down to The Lighthouse bar? They both started laughing. Panatine says, Poor old Cushion.

Never felt so bad, burn out your mind those drugs, the old man goes.

Well you asked what medication I was on, says Panatine.

Aye, I just had a wee cold though!

The Panatine began laughing and snorting beer then he
says, I was tripping away in the house after you'd left so
I thought I'd make it to the bottom of the hill for a drink
in The Lighthouse. I'm going down the brae, dancing
with the atoms, then I see this crawling smudge coming
up the pavement towards me out of the dark. As I get
closer it looks like a man with a leg missing, pulling himself along the pavement with his fingers; and thats what
it is, poor old Cushion pulling himself homeward.

Aye. Yon stuff made me feel so strange I left the pub
and walked along the esplanade. Thing is I believed I had
my leg back and I could walk, so I took off my false leg
and hurled it out into the water. I can still see it spinning
round and round with my shoe on the end; my best shoe
too, says Cushion.

Everyone was in the hysterics and smiling.

Tell the young ones here how you killed your wife,
Panatine shouted.

Cushion says, Laughs Like Water was her name girls.
I was a trapper in The Territories. Laughs Like Water.
Finest squaw I ever had. We had made camp when this
big bear run across the clearing. I picked up the gun,
followed the bear across in my sights, like this, then
slowly squeezed the trigger as I swung the gun round and
Bang. I blew Laughs Like Water's head off. Her whole
head just turned into a red dust and I can still see the rusty

cloud of it blowing away across the clearing and settling in the snow. I had to dig for two days to bury her in the frozen ground then the wolves took her the third night.

Lanna had gone awful pale. The Commander came over to our table.

How are the tides the night, shouted Red Hanna, standing and shaking hands with him.

No so bad, oh no so bad Mr Callar thank you. I just came to wish you all a happy new year. I cannot stop for a drink, I'm expecting two puffers in from the island with a hundred head of reindeer each so I've got to clear the pier.

Off he waddled and everyone kept in their hysterics till he passed the window.

It's a shame, I says to Red Hanna.

Suppose so. Have you set a date for your driving test?

I nodded and smiled. Red Hanna was looking at Lanna who was leaning across the table. He says, Your Lanna's grown into a lovely looking girl, eh?

I nodded.

It's right enough, Coll was saying, see that new ferry, yon foreign shipyard built the hull of too thick a steel. When it arrived here it was so unstable they had to cut it in half and weld thirty foot of thinner steel in the middle.

The Hiphearan came over to join our group. As well as two big tumblers of whisky he was holding a superstore carrier bag. You noticed a big fresh fish with its gaping mouth and an eye up against the greyish plastic was inside.

Well Hiphearan, a long time till High Season, says Coll.

Aye. Indeed. The Hiphearan took a swallow. His complexion was right roary from the bolting of nips. We'll maybe get a hot spell just at Easter there, he says.

It must have been well beyond licensing hours cause Strathclyde's Finest marched in and started throwing people out. A sergeant came up to the Glory Hole and says, Leave the premises now please.

Folk started to move outside with their pint glasses but a policewoman was collecting them all at the door.

Oh, cmon, happy new year or what, Panatine bawled out.

The Hiphearan had three glasses of whisky and was arguing with the sergeant who was telling him to leave the drinks and get out. You could see how loath The Hiphearan was to part with his nips. Suddenly The Hiphearan lifted the big fish out the carrier bag then poured each glass of whisky into the mouth of the fish. Then with all the railway and others cheering he carried the fish past the police and outside; The Hiphearan put the fish-mouth up to his own and tilted it back, drinking out all the whisky from its insides.

You saw The Panatine was over at a waiting taxi then he climbed up onto the roof, buckling it all in and with a boot sent the plastic mini-cab sign flying over the sea wall. Sure enough it was The Skiabhanach inside.

Strathclyde's Finest started haring in, but the taxi suddenly drove forward and accelerated. Panatine had the gumption to get down on his stomach and hang on, spread-eagled on the roof as the car sped away towards

The Mantrap with the police running after and a gang behind them all in hysterics. Just down by the north pier the car did a really good handbrake-skid and you saw The Panatine's body go turning in the other direction and hit the road. Then the rain started coming down in sheets. The Kale Onion began serving again but Lanna led me and The Bakery Girls up towards The Mantrap.

The Panatine was being loaded in the ambulance across from The Mantrap and everyone had stopped dancing to come out and watch. The Panatine was laughing and one of the ambulance men was shaking his head and saying to the police, It's him again, it's him.

Cause of rain, folk were going back in The Mantrap. The Bakery Girls moved off to start first-footing but Lanna and me walked quickly up past Video Rental and St John's then the Phoenix and Bayview till we were in the street below the windows and skylights of my flat.

When we got into the corridor I glanced up at the loft hatch with the padlock I'd put on. Lanna walked straight through saying, I havent been here in donks. Youve still all His stuff! Oh Morvy, my head's buzzing with this tab.

I locked the door and put out the corridor light cause of first-footers plagueing. I lit another of those incense cones then says, You're soaken wet. Cmon we'll have a bath. I put on the immerser and the bar fire. When I got the Christmas tree going at a medium sort of flash, Lanna put her face in her hands so I slowed it right down. She started looking at all His bookshelves.

Whats this? Lanna says.

69

I glanced over and went, It's an encyclopaedia; a sort of hardback about everything. What music do you want on?

Some of His stuff.

No want some 'core; those DJs?

Nut. Put some of His queer records on, Lanna says.

I goes, I really reckon I'll put this tape of the DJs on, and I put it in.

Morvy!

No Lanna, theres a reason.

Aw honeybunch sorry, does His stuff remind you of Him?

Nut, nut it's no that. His records and CDs are the only thing I wont be sending off to the auction rooms one Saturday. The tape started the playing. Out of a swirly synth these buzzing bleeps that could have been samples offof old Moogs but they set up a groove then it was insinuated slowly: that real Darkside theme and the heavy bass drum started, echoed by a syn-drum. A trance pulse locked on before the fanfare break then it all kicked together with a second bass then the clear girl voices singing the eerie theme: I Feel So Happy For No Reason At All. Lanna was up, legs slightly splayed, swishing her fingers to and fro by her eyelashes and jerking out her hip so all the beads clicked together down her front and I grabbed her and giggled, Nah, nah Lanna, look.

Out His desk drawer I took a folder with the travel agent name on it.

What is it? Lanna says.

It's for you and me.

What is it then?

Thats why I've got this tape on. We've got to see Creeping Jesus about changing your holidays. I've booked us both a fortnight in July at a resort, Youth Med. Dont be worrying about the money, He gave me a little when He left, thats what I wanted to really get you up here to tell you. Also Lanna, theres something else I have to tell you.

What? she whispered.

You can move in here with me. No right away mind, I've got some right clearing out of old junk to do, but say after we come back from the resort.

Morvern.

What? I put my hand on her shoulder.

Youre just so awful lovely to me and, I mean theres no reason, but youre so good.

Shush dafty.

He left you money?

I says, Aye a bit. Cmon. Bath.

Everything came off and Lanna got in first saying, Oh these bubbles are crazy.

Still tripping? I says.

Aye. Tripping like anything. It's getting heavier, she goes.

You'll be fine here.

You should take that other one and we'll be okay. We could watch all your weirdy horror films.

I says, Is that water burny?

Cant tell.

I put my bare leg in and says, Lanna it's pretty freezing. Move toes.

I poured in more hot. Better?

Thats ample; thats suffish, says Lanna.

I climbed in but had to let a bit out the plughole to stop it overflowing.

When we were dried through in the front room Lanna sat with my leg in her hands angling my knee around under the light till she got all the sparkles off it. Then I sat with Lanna's foot in my lap using the pedicure set she gave me. I put the toe-dividers between her toes and she kept giggling. I painted each toenail Emerald Sky with a squiggly line of Silver Starlite through it. Then Lanna goes, Hey! Let's go up the loft and play on the model village at night.

I looked up. Nah, not a good idea.

Oh come on, it would be brilliant tripping.

I smiled and says, Are you really out your face?

Aye. It would be hysterical seeing the trains go round.

No. I've took it all to bits for selling, I says.

Let's do a bit baking then, goes Lanna.

Eh? I laughed.

Cmon two-ton-tess, went Lanna jumping up and opening all the scullery cupboards.

You'd better get some clothes on you. I'd've thought you'd enough of baking at that place.

Wheres the flour; what butter've you got? says Lanna,

kneeling down sudden so's you saw her slim hips widen out. She switched on the oven.

I got the flour and there were new butters in the fridge.

Lanna says, Is it plain flour? Oh goody cause self-raising tends to puff up and go hard. Do you have any caster sugar?

She measured out on the old scales getting me to check; about a kilo flour then all the 250g butter block with a tablespoon of caster sugar got put in the big Pyrex. Lanna started scrunching and crumbling, letting it all fall through her fingers. Flour was right up her arms on the tiny hairs and every time she lifted a hand to touch away some hanging hair from her face she got flour on her nose or cheeks. You were just in hysterics watching her there.

This is the way to do it; with millions of butter so's it's creamy as anything, says Lanna.

I sprinkled in some water to moisten up the pastry till Lanna goes, Thats ample.

She sprinkled flour on the formica then battered the big pastry blob down. When she spread some flour along the rolling pin Lanna quickly threw the wee-bit-leftovers at me. I screamed and grabbed a big handful out that went all over her. A big flour fight started with us both going in total hysterics till we were pale from clouds of it exploding and settling on surfaces.

We both looked the colour white the way He had looked, lying above in the darkness when the snow had settled down on Him.

Lanna started rolling the dough out in one direction

then another so's it got thinner and she says, Have you a tray for making wee pies or a pastry cutter?

Nut, what'll we make then? I goes.

Whatever we'll need to pat it and prick it and then put it in the oven for Morvern Callar and me, says Lanna.

We both laughed, her mouth seeming right deep and darkish cause of the whiteishness of faces.

I'm never going to be able to eat any of this, I says.

She cut little bases and made walls and tops that stood up on a metal tray. She painted them in egg. They were full of jam.

Look, your hand is shaking, says Lanna.

I looked at it and it was.

We put the tarts in the oven. Lanna clapped her hands together causing flour to drift about.

Let's have a dance, I goes.

Lanna chose one of His records. It was Prince doing The Future. Our hands were the fingery movements of voices that set the theme, weaving in and out then splitting up, shooting out half the theme just to remind you. Thighs and middle were the throbbing you hear cushioning it all. Feet chose to move as you felt: to the percussion or the broken up words, then Lanna and me did a daft little waltz to the orchestra bit that sounded jiggled about. Our eyes looked at each other and we tried to do a tango.

Lanna jumped and put on my PM Dawn doing Set Adrift On Memory Bliss offof Of The Heart, Of The Soul And Of The Cross: The Utopian Experience. Lanna was going Dum Da Da Da Da. We had a slowish dance then Lanna says, I better fold out the couch.

I folded it down and got some sheets out the boiler cupboard. You heard Lanna turning the music down a bit.

When she was all tucked in I says, The oven. I switched it off.

We can have them for breakfast, Lanna went.

Night night, I goes.

Through the bedroom I lay down. The Beautiful by PM Dawn was going, quiet. After a bit Lanna appeared in the door. Morvy my head's freaking me, she says, getting under the downie.

It's nice like this. Dont like sleeping alone, I says.

Mmm, she went. Lanna turned and her breath was going below my collar bone. She put one arm over and round and the other under. Then we were lying on our backs with my mouth by the soft-feelingness of her neck, smelling of flour.

Lanna, I whispered.

What?

Happy new year.

She shoved up on her elbows in the darkness and goes, Aye happy new year honeybunch.

There was a bit of silentness then she says, Thanks Morvern, and put the fingers of a hand in her mouth the way she always fell asleep and I must have soon after.

All was as per usual till open-skylight-days, then actual heatwave come to the port. It was the day of my driving test and I'd got my period. High Season was starting and up The Complex all windows would be open with curtains hanging and moving a bit in breeze. Wee ones would be mucking about with buckets of water on the pavements. Even if you were way up among the hazy whins you would hear the ice cream van in The Complex below. If you climbed till you could see over, you would look at sea all the colour blue then greener as far as the island.

During the week at lunchbreak I had took a summerbag so's I could get in a short dress and sunglasses. I'd walk up and down the seawall with an ice pole or nicked fruit from the fridges. Some shopgirls with nowhere to change at work would dash up to their parents' place in The Complex and get into a blouse and short skirt just to give them a half hour in sunglasses, parading in groups up and down the busy esplanade. Gangs of office boys and mechanics would be leaning against the seawall with their jackets off or sleeves rolled up, drinking cans of juice. These boys would eye up the passing shopgirls and any female holidaymakers. The boys would know the names of the local girls and they'd argue what ones were Boots and what ones were Rides; unless someone's sister passed when there would be no talking. The boys would ask to meet at the first, second or third bench up Jacob's Ladder. There were arguments about the highest bench cause it gave a view over the bay and from the first one you just saw the bricks of the distillery chimney. I'd been on every level over the years and plummed for the top one any day with the smell of hops rising as hands were let up the skirt.

After shop-closing time when the warmth of the sun had gone the girls who had paraded at lunchtime would go up The Complex in their uniform or morning clothes with the lunchtime summer-wear in a plastic bag.

Though I'd my period it wasnt Ramraider so I wore a short dress and actual stockings. Sometimes I get a bit oily shine on my T-zone area so all I used was a light-medium shaded base to get a matt finish and some super-fine translucent powder.

I met the guy at the government buildings.

Not a bad day, eh?

Lead me to the vehicle please, the guy says.

In the car he tested my eyesight on a numberplate. He always says everything like he was reading from a book.

In first then in second, letting him see that I was using the mirror, we circled the station square. I changed up using the mirror at the overtaking and trying not to let him notice me licking my lipstick to keep it shiny.

Changed down smoothly by the Gathering Halls, down the Golden Mile and St John's Square and past the super-store from where I'd got the day off. Three-point-turn outside the clubhouse. On the way back the guy advised me then hit the dash. I put my foot right down on the brake and pumped it a little till we did a firm stop with no hint of skid.

The Give Way, indicate right at The Mantrap, left at

The Kale Onion, reversing round a corner, hill-start below the circular folly.

Just at the top of Jacob's Ladder I slowed right down. Two dogs were doing it in the middle of the road.

Move round . . . the obstruction please, he says.

There wasnt room and the stuck-together-dogs wouldnt budge.

Sound the horn and move round the obstruction please.

I beeped the horn and the dogs shifted awkwardly. I revved up and changed into second. When we did a right onto the straight by Couris Jean's I stole a look at the guy. He was smiling and looking at me. You could tell we were both trying not to go into hysterics and he says quietly, Just keep going, youre really doing well.

A driving tester was never meant to say this to you so you just realised that I was going to get my licence and drive out the port for ever. I didnt look at him when he says this and though I'd saw him dart a look at the creaminess of skin under the black low-denier stocking you knew he was an okay sort.

We rounded the corner onto Burnbank Terrace and you could see the phone box down at the end just beyond the bit under my windows below an open-skylights-day sky.

His clipboard jerked forward and hit the dashboard. I stood on the brake with the clutch out so the tyres let out a loud scream as the engine juddered and stalled completely while my dress pushed right up.

There were men in orange jackets working up on the roof.

I undid the seatbelt, stepped out the car and jerked down the fankled dress. A car was honk-honking behind. The driving tester leaned over and switched the Hazard Warning Lights on; he was staring at me.

I've failed eh? sorry I'm really carsick I must go now, I says. I horsed it to the door at the close. The guy got out the car and shouted, Wait.

I went pelting up the stairs, tried to put the keys in to get the door opened. Inside I'd to waste seconds locking the door behind me cause the driving tester was the kind might follow you to see what was wrong.

I dragged over a scullery stool, jumped on it and unlocked the loft hatch. I hauled the hatch down with the hook then booted the stool away. I felt the stockings tear as my shins got banged going up the ladder. It stunk in there. I let down the ratchets. His body slowly wound down on the base from the bright blueishness of open skylights. I tore the tight dress off over my head, tugging and grunting till it came away. I leapt up on the model and on tiptoe, the same way I could just kiss His forehead, I could just peer out the gap in the skylight. The men in jackets the colour orange were fixing the slates way down at the next chimney. They must never've been near the skylights. I jumped down and got some sheets from the bedroom. I climbed back up and flung the sheets over Him then got down on my knees and started greeting cause of failure of the driving test. The door intercom buzzed for a few minutes but I kneeled there greeting in big heaves till it was afternoon when I got changed and walked down the town to the ironmongers.

I swallowed down the tab with a glass of Remy Martin and a swig Heineken. The period pain was going away when I came out the darkness bare-naked into the glare of the reflector light above the bath. I was holding the new meat knife and the gardening saw; I kneeled down to him and put on the gloves.

I couldnt see too much. I was wearing all my hair under a tight fleshy coloured swimming cap. I had on reddish-tinted swimming goggles, and noseclips attached to a fluorescent string were on my nostrils. Round my bare tummy was that studded belt and the Walkman clipped to it with the plugs Sellotaped into my ears.

I'd recorded a suitable compilation:

Track Listing:

SIDE A	SIDE B
Last Exit: Straw Dog.	Ronald Shannon Jackson
You Got Me	and The Decoding
Rockin'.	Society: Undressing.
Take Cover.	Luciano Berio: Visage.
Ma Rainey.	Miles Davis: Pharaoh's
Crack Butter.	Dance.
Panzer Be Bop.	Ronald Shannon Jackson:
Miles Davis: Great	Taboo.
Expectations.	Challenge To Manhood.

Sonny Sharrock: Dick   Bill Laswell: Assassin.
Dogs.

I cut away the still-hanging hand and sliced into the
first arm. The coloured goggles helped take away the
reality of what you were up to and you didnt smell a
thing with those tight noseclips that would do fine for
Lanna on holiday too.

What you do is divide the limbs and wrap them in a
good few layers of binliner and absorbent hessian sacking
bound again and again with strips of thick parcel tape.
There wasnt that much blood till at one part I pushed
down heavily on a portion and a jet scooshed up from a
dry-looking vein and trickled off my bosoms and front
getting on to my thighs. I'd not bothered with a Tampax
and you saw that my own blood had in fact been running
down my leg and drops were on the newspapers mingling
with His while I worked on.

You dont get difficulty with the head or limbs, it's the
organs pushing out from the torso sodden through with
blood. The two torso packages needed almost twice as
much wrapping but I made a good job of them. I stashed
the easy-to-handle packages in the loft. After scrubbing
and a bath I came into the front room and sat at His desk.
I opened the drawer and took out the computer disc. I
switched on and inserted the disc in drive A.

MY FATHER DIED, HA! SORRY JUICY FRUIT. I HAVE DECIDED

TO PLAY THIS PRANK ON MYSELF. KEEP ME ON MY TOES. I *WAS* HAPPY WITH YOU MORVERN BUT THINGS BECAME TOO CUSHY FOR THIS OLDEST OF CHANCERS. I WAS ALWAYS LOOKING FOR PEACE BUT HERE, YOU TAKE IT INSTEAD. EVERYTHING HAS BEEN ARRANGED, HANG AROUND HERE A FEW MONTHS.

MY NOVEL IS ON THIS DISC. PRINT IT OUT AND SEND IT TO THE FIRST PUBLISHER ON THE LIST I'VE MADE. IF THEY WILL NOT TAKE IT TRY THE NEXT. I ONLY ASK YOU TO GET IT PUBLISHED. I'LL SETTLE FOR POSTHUMOUS FAME AS LONG AS I'M NOT LOST IN SILENCE.

I LOVE YOU MORVERN; FEEL MY LOVE IN THE EVENINGS IN THE CORNERS OF ALL THE ROOMS YOU WILL BE IN. KEEP YOUR CONSCIENCE IMMACULATE AND LIVE THE LIFE PEOPLE LIKE ME HAVE DENIED YOU. YOU ARE BETTER THAN US.

I DON'T WANT TO LEAVE THIS LIFE WHICH I LOVE SO MUCH. I LOVE THIS WORLD SO MUCH I HAVE TO HOLD ONTO THIS CHAIR WITH BOTH HANDS.

NOW SEND OFF THIS NOVEL AND HAVE NO REMORSE. BE BRAVE.

RIGHT NOW, TO WORK!

X X X X X

After a good while I started paging forward through the disc. This novel thing was page after page of words then a number then more pages of words and another number. You had to read to get to the end; you couldnt see the point in reading through all that just to get to an end.

Without reading a word of it I toddled over to the video and put on The Thing, not the original but the re-make with special fx. When it was half way through I put it on Pause. I stood up and walked around the room. I sniffed a few times and looked at the clock on the video. I sat down and the coloured light from the computer screen was on the tops of my two hands that lay on the desk.

It was the first page of the novel that was up on display. You saw His name and below it words. You presumed they must be the name of the novel: its Title. And the different numbers, they would be: Chapters.

I lifted my face up staring at the colours on the screen. Then I was looking at His name.

My fingers touched the keys and typed letters over His name.

I switched on the laser printer and typed in:

SHIFT-F7, FI, I

I had to go to the cupboard to get all the paper and load the printer.

The pages came whizzing out onto the tray.

I set the rest of The Thing going and moved my neck from side to side as if I was easing the muscles.

When The Thing had ended and the video was winding back I gathered the pages in both hands and knock-knocked them on the edge of the desk to bring the wad flush together. I put the stack of pages on the scullery table and you saw what I had typed over the words of His name on the first page of that novel:

BY MORVERN CALLAR.

I WAS DOWN on my hunkers cupping up cold river water and dashing it on my face. I grit teeth at coldness of the water though the heatwave was still a real scorcher and you could feel the sun hot on your hair.

When I'd sat on the dry boulder and got my legs warm enough in the sun so's there were no goosebumps I creamed the foam on and shaved them with the Bic. I put the razor on a rock then stepped into the shallow clear water and scooped more up over my thighs and shins. My toes ached after too long in the river. Back on the boulder I dried my legs on the towel and used the moisturiser. It was so warm in the sun I let out a big shivery gasp when I got back in the stream with the soap and chucked water up between my legs and round my bottom. I rubbed up a thick lather then splashed up more water, watching the suds immediately dash away round rocks. When I paddled across shallow pools and streamlets carrying the wet towel, I tried not to put my feet on slimy bits then hopped up on the grass of the low sandy riverbank.

I sat with my legs in the sun and unpacked the pedicure set. I put the toe-dividers in then re-coated all toenails in

Dusky Cherry that looked bright against the grass. When the toenails were dry I put on the leather sandals then unhooked the chopped-off jeans from the birch tree twigs and stepped into them. I put the nail varnish and toe-dividers back in the pedicure bag but I just left the other toilet things out on the boulder for next morning. I hung the towel up on the branch and put the T-shirt on. I walked upstream along the bank and past the toilet I'd dug near the sand so's you could sprinkle some in every time you paid a visit.

I kneeled to the little pool made by the three stones that trapped my bottles in the cold running water. I fished out the plastic bottle with milk in and two hard boiled eggs from the night before.

That T-shirt was the colour green with two little pockets at the front. The boiled eggs bumped against my chest, dangling in the wee pockets, and I held the milk in one hand then with one palm on my bare thigh pushed up the steep brae to the tent.

I drank what you could spare of the milk then chapped the eggs on those stones I'd lugged up from the river to put round the fire. One blackened stone had cracked and another had a fuzz of oxide on it. I'd got a fair bleeze going the night before so's to keep midges at bay.

I used the goldish lighter on a Silk Cut and peered at Beinn Mheadhonach. The haze was lifting, turning into pure heat, but a breeze was managing to get up too; the breeze would be stronger on the high turning braes up the side of the mountain. Over the river the first slopes were brindled with heather.

I flicked eggshell into the ashes then crawled in the tent for the salt. It was a furnace inside so's I got the Walkman out as well.

I'd made up a compilation tape that I knew would suit the camping weekend in such heatwave.

Track Listing:

SIDE A	SIDE B
Salif Keita: Nyanafin.	The Can: Future Days.
Les Têtes Brûlées et	Holger Czukay: Persian
Zanzibar: Essingan.	Love.
This Mortal Coil:	The Can offof Ege
Another Day.	Bamyasi Okraschoten:
The Ink Spots: Up A	Pinch.
Lazy River.	Sing Swan Song.
The Cocteau Twins:	Vitamin C.
Blue Bell Knoll.	Soup.
Material: Disappearing.	I'm So Green.
	Spoon.

I put on the Walkman and changed into the socks and boots. With the mirrored shades on I zipped up the tent then ran sideways down the brae to pop the milk back in the pool.

I stepped over to the whin bush then reached in behind the spikeys and the flesh-soft yellowy cups of petals. The big plastic backpack I'd left the last week was there with a stone and large trowel sat on top.

I hopped from stone to stone across the river not getting the boots wet. I climbed the sheep-path into a spread of fresh, bright-coloured bracken then I pushed my way to the middle bringing up a plague of flies round my head. I just used the goldish lighter on a Silk Cut, exhaling big puffs. I peered over but you couldnt see the backroad through the jittering leaves of the birches.

Using the trowel I scraped away rich-smelling soil. There were no other smells. When I heard the scratching noise I tugged at the buried cardboard box but it was damp and tore. I leaned in then lifted out the roundish package of binliner and parcel tape. I dumped it into the plastic backpack, stood up and used my foot to kick the scraps of damp cardboard and the excavated soil back in the shallow hole. I dropped the trowel in the backpack then started hunching it up on my shoulders so it was sitting as comfy as possible on my back. Soil was all under my nails like at work. I rubbed hands on the bum of the chopped-off jeans in a nonplussed way.

To the happy sound of Salif Keita doing Nyanafin I rounded the great bank of Beinn Mheadhonach, pushing down on my tanned legs. The sun was hot on my hair as His chopped-off head bumped away against my back.

My boots pushed in the soft pinkish mounds of moss, and moor cotton buds tipped over whenever a breeze came. I climbed staring at the moss and tawny grass, missing the odd buds of saxifrage with my feet.

I stopped the going-up every time my heart was really banging in my throat and you could feel prickles of sweat under the backpack. I kept climbing and the mountainside eased over so when you turned you saw the whole land below. The land was flattening out I was getting so high up and a hot haze had appeared in the clear bright light of the morning.

Salif Keita sounded so good in the sunshine I stuck out my arms and started spinning round slowly, squinting up at the sun so it looked to be darting and was warm in the face. I was dizzy when I stopped. You saw the tiny tent far down beyond the rounded slopes I was stood on. Then my eyes followed the river down to the rigs and policies where it poured into the loch. Lumpy outcrops of grass mounds hung flared with birches over the path of the river's fall to lower ground. I made to sit down but the moss squelched so I jumped back up.

As I rounded the side so's you could see the actual top, Blue Bell Knoll was going in my ears. I took out the head and put it down a good bit away. I made special sure it was secure then laughed out loud in case it went rolling and bouncing all the way back down with me chasing. I shoved it a bit into the heather, pushing down on the bin liner and the parcel tape.

I took off the mirrored shades and, using the trowel, I scraped and tugged at the tough grass and mosses till I gouged out some soil. In those mountains it was easy to come against rock dead quick so's I'd chosen a dip like that where you could be sure of some peaty soil. The hole filled up with water that was the colour black and stained my arms up to the elbows.

I dropped the head inside the backpack then shoved the pack in the hole. I scooped biggish blobs of muck on top and pressed the lot down. You could hear bubbling as the backpack under filled with water. I put the clods on top the delve and gave it all a good thumping down with my feet. I held my arms out for a while to let the mud just dry on the skin then I climbed on up swinging the trowel to I'm So Green till I came to the big gathering of tons boulders with soil and mosses capping the tops. I climbed up on the one, used the goldish lighter on a Silk Cut and switched off the Walkman.

From up there you could see all that land; from the Back Settlement westwards where the railway moved into the pass, following the road toward the power station, the village beyond where the pass widened out towards the concession lands. Birches clustered in sprays where the dried-up burns dipped into the streams. One stream ran under the concrete bridge by the sycamore where sweet primroses were spreading thickly. Flickers were coming off the loch and the massive sky seemed filled with a sparkling dust above those hot summer hills, fattened with plants and trees. You could hear the water-falls down in the gulley. They would be spraying onto ferns there and drops of water would be hanging from their tips. I looked out at the landscape moving without any haste to no bidding at all. I yawned a big yawn. Two arms and a leg were buried on the cliff above the sycamore tree and higher up the torso and leg would be helping flower the sheets of bluebells below the dripping rocks. All across the land bits of Him were buried.

I stood and stretched then put the Walkman on. I looked around me as if to see what was on the agenda. I jumped off the boulder then started leaping down the slopes, watching like a hawk for any surprise cliffs.

I ran across the slope, my ankles getting whipped at by the wee heads of moor cotton, then on the lower slopes I began to get the giggles I was going so fast with bracken whacking my thighs so's I slashed out with the trowel.

I was out of puff when I slowed down. In the creamy shade of the birch trees a breeze flipped up the leaves showing their silvery undersides, and the sun trilling through flicked shadows on my face.

When I got to the river I lay on my tum-tum and stuck both arms in. The dried mud turned runny then floated off. Little hairs on my arms stood all erect.

Across the river I climbed up to the tent and chucked down the trowel that I would bury when I filled in the toilet.

I walked down by the river with the orangey dress then peeled off the T shirt, the chopped-off jeans and put the dress on. I dunked the muddy clothes in the water and rung them out then I hung them on the branches from where I tugged off the towel then headed downstream.

I was hopping from boulder to boulder, balancing then quickly jumping forwards. The river widened into a curve, falling down in steps towards the loch. I stopped moving forwards. The rock I was on was a bit wobbly. I stepped onto another. In front of me a giant stone leaned against the bank that had collapsed in a side of sand and little boulders. A dam higher than me had built up against the giant stone, driving the water over onto an angled face that cradled the flow into a massive ambery-coloured rock-pool. Water poured out the pool in a wide rush down another load of stone steps.

I climbed over the sandy side, swung down round some birch trunks then chucked the towel on the flat stone by the pool. I took off the Walkman, put it down, folded the towel then tugged up the dress over my head. I unlaced the boots and walked down into the pool; shivering I stumbled deeper, gasping as water splashed up on my chest, then I ducked under and put my head out, shaking the strings of cold water from my hair and kicking across to the deep bit. Gritty stuff was in my mouth.

You couldnt swim straight ahead for long before having to circle. I treaded water a bit and my legs looked greeny then browny when deeper under the surface. My breath was a bit shuddery and beads of water were darting off my shoulder. I kicked over to some polished branches jammed where the water tipped out the pool. I hung on one then an insane-looking dragonfly buzzed fast over the water. Some berries that were the colour black floated round and round behind a piece of rock so I splash-splashed them over into the current and they whizzed away. I swum over to the flat rock then climbed out, feeling for stone in case I chipped my toenails on it. I bent my head and squeezed water out my hair. It splattered on my feet and the dusty rock. I sat down on the towel in-the-scud and got my legs stretched out. It was stifling hot and you saw the wet footprints and splashes drying. I looked at the drops of water on my skin then squinted up when the breeze moved the trees above the pool. I used the goldish lighter on a Silk Cut then lay back and shut my eyes. I kept like that till the rock was sore through the towel then I turned over. I dozed a bit in the heat then sat up on my elbows and set the Walkman going, leaning and just looking straight ahead at nothing special. There was a birch leaf and you could see the bright fresh streak of a birdy-dropping on it. I smoked another Silk Cut and tried to tap the ash off without breaking it up. The little tubes of ash tumbled about and crumbled on the rock as breeze came.

The sun had moved round the sky and the air was cooler by the pool when I stood up. There were long marks down my front from lying on the rock. I stretched and a gust across the water made the first goosebumps come. I got the dress on and rubbed grit off my feet. I tied up the laces yawning, then moved back upstream gathering shiny branches.

When I got to the tent I threw the shiny branches into the ashes. Sunset was starting. I tore tiny twigs and cones from a branch in the big heap I'd gathered the weekend before. The twigs and cones were so tinder-dry you could just set fire to them using the goldish lighter. A few thinner branches on top got a good strong heart in the

bleeze. I saw juicy sap from one twig bubbling and popping out from its torn end, then a little jet of smoke
rings came puttering out before the end flared up and sap
dripped into the red hot embers underneath. More twigs
got piled on, crackling up and glowing bright till they
turned to white tubes and fell in. The smoke shot straight
up into the still-bright sky. It was fairly blazing so's I
dragged across the log I'd been saving with the long
branch on it. I put it so the sticking out bits you couldnt
break off were across the flames. A cloud of red hot
cinders shot up.

Down the river I filled the billy can. Kneeling over the
water, sunset going on, everything was luminous. When
taking the billy can up the brae I held out one arm to
balance me. I could hear the fire's crackle before I came
up over the grassy bank. I hung the billy can, shifting it
so the tips of flames ended just under its bottom.

Back down the river you could smell smoke in my hair
when I fished out the margarine and milk. With the gentle
light from above and the pitch black trees in front of me,
coming back up the brae was like being held in a big
purple glove.

Midges were starting so I walked away from the fire
and tore up green bracken, caw-cannying not to slash my
fingers on stalks. I used the stick to lift the billy can off
the flames using both my hands and tottering a bit. The
sticky-out branch on the log had burnt away. With the
toe of my boot I gave the trunk a sharp shove into the

heart then jumped back as sparks shot up. I layered the bracken on top so's it began to put out an oily smoke.

When I looked up from the sipping of the coffee, shaky blobs of stars were pushing out above me. The pasta was boiled enough so I held the lid at the rim with my towel then lay the billy can on its side. Starchy water drained out through the little holes and I plopped in a blob of margarine. The low-burned fire was good for cooking. I fried the chopped-up onion, tinned tomats and kidney beans with burger mix. The heat was on my cheeks so much, when you turned away you felt coolness. I tipped up the billy can and the pasta slid out and bubbled with the sauce. I ate straight out the pan. I blew steam from my mouth every now and then when I got a hot bit. I took the odd swig from the milk bottle. The sky was dark and sheets of stars were trembling above me.

I lit a Silk Cut off embers then gazed into the fire. It'd died down and the cinders tinkled. The light from the fire was throwing out less and less shadow round the tent. The dark outline of all the mountains was round me. The butt of a Silk Cut lit up in the ashes. A shadow wobbled by the tent. I yawned and there was a buzzing in my ears. I unzipped the front of the tent then crawled in.

Birds were singing and I pushed aside the flap. You could smell the night leaving the earth and everything waking. An ancient-looking sun was drumming up the loch and offof the water. Another scorcher starting. I climbed out the tent and stretched my hands-to-the-high-sky. I put on the sandals and walked down to the river in my jammy bottoms.

I threw water up in my face and didnt dry though cold drops dripped down. When I brushed my teeth I was standing up in the sun squinting at the high ridges where I'd seen three deer the last weekend. Three deer, standing, looking right at me.

I carried all the cooking things down to the water and rinsed the billy can out. Some pale bits of conchiglie pasta floated away round the rocks and were carried through the pools and streamlets. I cleaned out the empty cans then scoured the saucepan with clumps of grass before dunking it in the current.

I filled the billy can and climbed the brae, one arm out holding the saucepan, then piled more sticks on the dusty ash to set a fire going.

I drank two cups coffee quick then made another. I walked slowly down the brae and set up on a boulder with my Silk Cuts and goldish lighter. It was already lunchtime, you could see from the position of the sun. After smoking a couple I hopped the stones to my toilet bag and took out the shampoo. I crossed and unhooked the towel giving it a good shake. I'd just got to the stones and was starting to move downstream when I heard it.

I jerked my head up and did a big breath. Kicking out

sheets of splashes I crossed to the bank where you heard it again, queerly distinctive in the glen the way you can distinguish moonlight from streetlight in the port.

I took a run at the brae and was panting up the top. In front of the tent I tipped the billy can water onto the fire and there was a whoosh of sudden steam. I pulled on a T-shirt then in the tent got the little denim skirt. When I crawled out the tent I sighed. I could even make out the words the voice was echoing up the glen:

YOO HOO, MORVERN. YOO HOO. YOO HOO
MORVERN

I trudged up to the backroad. There was heat-haze far down the single track of tarmac; through it some colours smeared together. It looked like she was bouncing: she was on her bicycle.

Shaking my head I trotted down to the tent. Lanna was riding up over the concrete bridge, her thighs were taut, stood up as she was on the pedals. She sat on the saddle then came shaking down the bank, swishing through the bracken and screaming. She jumped off the bike as it was moving: it clunked down. Lanna kept running towards me and stopped so's I'd to take a step back.

Found you buggerlugs. I saw the smoke. Look at the tan youve got you holy terror; it's boiling, eh? she says.

How did you find me?

Your smoke, can see it miles back. I left the port before seven; it was a totally gorgeous morning. Red Hanna's at

97

V the D's so's I just cycled out and he goes that you were this way. He did me a map:

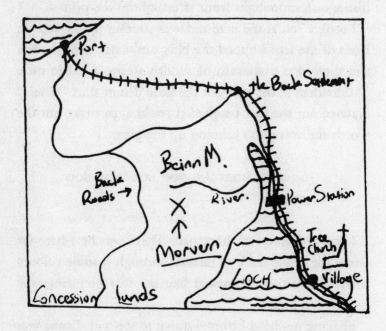

We walked in the tent direction.

My sweet arse is killing me; mustve cycled seven mile. Dont you get scared here? says Lanna looking up Beinn Mheadhonach.

What of?

Well, men could just come along and rape you.

What men? Theres two cars gone up the backroad since Friday night.

Dont you get the spooks on your own?

Nut, I goes.

What are you smiling at? Lanna says.

It's weird hearing my voice out loud, I goes.

Lanna looked about again and says, Well I would get the spooks. The hills have eyes, Granny Couris Jean says.

How is she?

I was over the other day and she was asking about you. I just told her that you were camping on your own every weekend and that we were away to a resort.

Do you want to come swimming cause I've to wash my hair? I says.

Is it not got biting fish in or clegs?

Nah, I goes grabbing the towel.

Using my fingers I smeared more fresh mud out the little hole and across Lanna's cheekbones. Her eyes looked mentally white with the blackishness of the muck round. I caked more onto her forehead then up into the hairline.

I knew this would be a good facepack when I saw it, digging my little toilet up round that bend, I says while Lanna wiped more wetter stuff on my dried mask then she squashed a few rowan berries and heather onto my forehead where it stuck. I fixed some berries on Lanna's cheeks.

Cmon, do the fertility dance, says Lanna.

We both leaped up and hunched over, circling and grunting in a dance. Lanna'd taken her top off and brownness blackishness was splattered down her tits.

Escape harmful rays with this remarkable Factor Twelve, goes Lanna flickering her eyes.

I laughed and it echoed back from the cliff.

We started moving downriver. Where the grass ended

in the bank of sand and pebbles at the river edge we stopped.

Now caw-canny on boulders cause if you fall you'll break your leg in a split second, I says.

We moved from boulder to boulder. I let Lanna go first. I watched her body from behind as she jumped, balanced; then jumped on. Sometimes her tits pulled up and almost disappeared when she held her hands out and moved her arms in a carousel as she yelped and tried to balance. I popped up on the stone beside her and we laughed into each's mud-pack-face. Lanna clung with an arm then leapt on.

When we got to the pool I chucked the towel on the flat rock.

This is pretty brilliant, goes Lanna.

I says, It's deep in the middle. See, if you keep your pumps on you could jump off up there into the deep bit.

Dare you then.

You too. Youre covered in it too ya mink.

We stripped off except for our feet then climbed up round the huge boulder and paddled across the deeper water with Lanna holding my hand. I tugged her up the other bank into long grass that tickled my shins.

I need to, Lanna says getting down among the grass and flowering sweet violet; her sharp, crouching bottom suddenly widened, outlined against the bright, then sparkling grass under her.

Up at me she says, I stopped at The Glue Pot for a lemonade.

I nodded.

We stepped out on the jutting rock. Lanna rested her mucky face on my shoulder, a berry fell off her cheek as she goes, Woops, you go first.

No ways; both together, I went.

We held hands and looked at each other. I says, Remember, right in the middle and dont go and do a bomber or you might hit rock, just keep legs straight, right . . .? ready to push off the bottom. The water'll slow us but it'll be really perishing so dont get a fright. Ready?

Lanna nodded.

We plucked up the courage then I goes, One,

Two,

Three.

We both screamed. Air moved past me. I turned my head, saw that with the hand that wasnt squeezing mine Lanna was gripping her nose.

We hit water. Coldness punched my chest and there was a boom. Lanna pulled her hand away. I opened my eyes and saw:

Bubbles, the copperishness of the water with big bars of sun going through and through.

I surfaced beside Lanna. The wave our splash caused was cupping against the cliff and sherbety bubbles were tickling up my thighs.

Again, again, bawled Lanna.

Oww it's freezing, I coughed out and pushed over to the warm rocks. I climbed out with my head held down, blackish drips fell on my bosoms: Blood, was what I obviously supposed and reached up with a finger. It was the mud running offof my face.

Lanna was doing doggy-paddle across the pool, her head held straight up in a funny way and big mud-shadows under her eye sockets.

Looking at her I laughed then swallowed.

I kneeled gently on my knees and pulled handfuls of water up into my face till there was no mud on me.

Cmon again, went Lanna from the other side of the pool where she was clung to a branch with her toes sticking out.

No ways, I goes.

Cmon. Cowardy ben, cowardy ben, bawled Lanna to egg me on.

I sat smoking Silk Cuts and watched Lanna's pale body appear through the birch trees and mellow shadows up by the jutting rock. Her freckles seemed to match the frills of bright sun being let through the leaves behind her. The ginger hair that turned blackish when wet was slapped in a rope over behind her back. She smiled down at me then jumped.

Lanna'd the elbow of the arm she squeezed her nose with firmly against her bosom. Her sandshoes pointed in a dainty way as she zipped into the water with a crack then came up with a deep laugh. She crawled out the pool with the water that dripped from her, hissing on the dusty rock.

We were quiet for a good bit just smoking. I got down

by the water then started shampooing my hair. Lanna watched, saying nothing.

I squeezed water out the hair then lay face down with my arms by my sides.

Lanna was sat in the shady bit under the big boulder smoking my Silk Cuts.

You could feel the heat rays on my skin but also bouncing off the rock next to my flesh.

The odd insect buzzed.

The water shushed away.

Breeze in leaves.

Birds.

I curled my fingers.

Really lazily Lanna says, Did you hear Shadow the shelf-stacker got given the boot from work? I reckon Creeping Jesus got sick of his gawkit face, fibbing and clipeing and burglarising with his thieving hands; I hated him he was a total perv.

Whats he doing for work? I mumbled.

Nothing. It's too late in the season for anything now. He says he was going to go out to work in the superquarry but theres no jobs there.

Dont talk about work Lanna, I cant face the thought of it tomorrow, I goes.

Youre the early eh?

Aye, I says and coughed.

There was a long bit of silentness. You heard wee splashes and when I squinted up you saw she was tossing pebbles in the pool. I put my head down again.

You missed yourself at The Mantrap last night, goes Lanna and she coughed. They had that real rubbish band on. The Panatine was heckling them then he just fell forward on his face unconscious and they couldnt shift him. He landed on those pedal things for the guitarist so's all these wild noises were coming out as he just lay there, Lanna laughed then coughed and was silent.

I moved my legs apart slow and felt the sun on the insides of my thighs.

It's a real all-over tan youve got, eh? Lanna says.

Aye, I goes.

I got my passport Friday, you should see my photo.

Sshh, I went.

Lanna gave a big huff.

The water shushed.

After a long time I says, Stay here a bit. In Nature. Away from Creeping Jesus and the work. This place, it doesnt care, it's just *here*. It helps that this place is here just a few hours' walk away. All this loveliness. It's just silence isnt it?

Aye it's fine in this weather. All year this river'll be rapids though, says Lanna chucking a really small pebble that didnt hit the water but tat, tat, tatted near my bare feet.

Morvern?

What?

I want to sort of tell you something.

What?

You'll be in a massive huff.

I pushed up on my elbows and squinted. What?

Lanna sighed and says, Know how we were bosom-pals?

Who us? I goes.

Nah, nah, me and Him.

Him?

Aye.

Aye, I goes.

Well we *were* bosom-bosom-pals.

What? I went.

You'll be in a massive huff, Lanna says.

There was a long long silentness and right high up in the sky you could hear a bird-sound moving away from the loch towards the mountains.

You dont know do you? says Lanna looking at me.

It was hard to speak when you were lay the way I was with my front stretched up. I goes, Did you go with Him then?

It was rubbish Morvern it was really rubbish.

I sat up but turned around away from her, sitting with my hands on my knees. I did a big breath. The feeling was going across me.

When? I goes.

That last afternoon you were working before Christmas, says Lanna.

The day before that party with the boys? I went.

Aye, goes Lanna. Then she says, It was useless.

Quiet. Dont talk. Please, I went.

There was such a long silentness in the warm afternoon

then Lanna didnt even move but says quietly, What are you going to do to me?

I shook my head and says, After all the making sure no tenderness could get taken by surprise. It still finds a way through all we did . . . and look at you. I turned round and looked at her. Lanna was staring at me.

I turned away and sobbed, chucking some snotter aside that stuck to the back of my wiping hand.

Dont cry, Lanna goes. She stood up but didnt move to me.

I turned my head round so I could see her and says, Tell me what things went on. Exact, I pointed and says, Here?

She was going to greet any minute.

I pointed and says, Here?

Lanna nodded.

What next?

She started pouring tears and hunching up.

WHAT, I bawled.

Just the usual Morvern, she goes.

So everything?

Aye.

Everything?

Aye, she goes and started the heavy greeting. It was rubbish though, she sort of shouted.

Did yous do that, I pointed.

Lanna nodded.

TELL ME.

From behind too, she admitted with her hand near her mouth.

How many did you use? I went.

Well, just one sort of.

There was a long bit of just the greeting sounds.

What do you mean sort of, did you use your mouth?

Not really.

WHAT DO YOU MEAN LANNA. TELL ME?

She says, We did it lots of times with nothing but He used one first shot and I looked at Him, I took the flunky off, I put my head back like this, tipped into my mouth and swallowed all that was inside just like The Hiphearan emptying the fish at Hogmanay. She started bubbling and greeting. I wanted to tell, she coughed, I wanted to tell, then when you says at Couris Jean's that He'd gone I left you sleeping and ran to your flat in the snow.

You went to the flat?

She nodded, I wanted to see Him but He was gone. I buzzed and buzzed. She started putting her clothes on with her bottom turned to me.

Get moving. Get out of here and dont dream of coming near me again, I says.

She nodded, then carrying her pumps she hoiked herself up round the rocks and out of sight.

Stepping out around the four-mile mark I was moving away from the pass. Where the backroad meets the main road the lorry tooted me and my hair moved in its wake. I started the walking over the lumpy, uneven verge.

You heard the cars coming up behind. I crossed to the safer side. Some cars had headlights on and the clean light made lots of sharp shadows in the grass at my feet. The noise of a car increased then it whipped past me and its noise faded, leaving the sound of the billy can handle squeaking where it hung on the pack behind me.

I passed the village name road sign:

BACK SETTLEMENT

I passed the 30 limit sign. Some kids hanging round outside the hotel stared at me and one shouted something dirty when I turned onto the road to the railway station. I stopped to turn back but when they scattered I just walked on. I crossed the humped railway bridge and V the D's bungalow was on the right.

Red Hanna was delving in the vegetable garden.

Did Lanna find you? Red Hanna shouted.

I nodded.

Stick the gear in the lean-to. Some day, eh?

Aye.

V the D materialised and goes, Oh Morvern, Morvern you must have sunstroke. My hayfever is awful I'll get you some juice.

Red Hanna walked up to me, Lanna find you aye?

Aye.

Aye well I guessed it'd be along opposite the power station. She was here at eight in the morning, I was still in bed. Vanessa was raging, you can imagine, he goes, nodding towards the open kitchen door.

Can you check if the train's on time? I says.

Well hold your horses, you just need to go down the path and ask whoevers in the box.

It doesnt matter, I goes.

Here, that Lanna's blossomed into a fair wee ginger-nutted cracker, says Red Hanna.

So youre fond of telling us, I goes, wrenching the billy can off then unbuckling the haversack. I pulled out the shoulder bag with my dirty clothes in it then I was out with the tent and shaking it.

Are you okay? went Red Hanna.

I put the haversack in their lean-to then folded the tent on top the bush by the turn in the path.

I carried the billy can in the scullery to try and wash it but V the D took it from me and plied me with juice. I stood in the doorway and shouted, Sorry I'm going to be away on holiday for your retirement do.

It's just going to be a wee thing Morvern, goes Red Hanna.

What are you doing? I says.

Nothing, just a wee drink at The Kale Onion on my last day. Backshift on my last day; can you believe it? he went.

Typical, I goes swallowing the diluted orange in two gulps.

I sniffed then says, I best get moving.

Have you not got a jacket with you or something girl? goes V the D.

Are you no stopping a minute longer; it's only twenty to, went Red Hanna.

They both looked at each other.

For goodness' sake Morvern, we've hardly seen you since Christmas, now we wont see you till youre back. We thought you might want a shot of the car to help you get Lanna's things down to your flat, I can sit in the car with you, says V the D.

Lanna's no moving in, I goes.

Oh whats the matter now, have yous had a fall out? went Red Hanna.

It's no really your business, I says looking at the grass.

Morvern youve to stop these huffs, went V the D.

Oh now leave her, goes Red Hanna.

Aye go depress someone else, I went.

Morvern, goes Red Hanna.

I'll see you on the train on the 16th, was the last thing I says.

I stepped over the wee low gate then turned up the single-track road that comes up from the slip on the loch. I crossed the railway bridge then turned down the path that was right overgrown that time of year.

Down on the platform a few older people from the village were just standing there to watch the train go through and see who came off it. The old ladies stared at me. I turned my back on them and out the shoulder bag I took the moisturiser and rubbed some into my snout.

It was getting a bit chilly for the short dress I'd on.

Then way down at the other end of the pass you heard the diesel climbing away from the Falls platform above the entrance to the power station. You heard the horn blow and that meant it was SPD driving who would be tooting as the train passed The Turbines Bar where he was going with one of the summer barmaids. I would ride on the engine with him.

Back in the flat just the sounds of me moving round on my own told a bleak story. There was a letter with a London postmark.

They wanted to publish my novel and would cover the expenses of me paying them a visit to talk to them. They would give me £1,875 if I signed that contract then £625 when the book was published. I looked at the floor for a time then it was a low long laugh I gave out.

The flat was a right midden but I searched for the things I'd need to write a letter:

Dear Tom Bonnington,

Heres that contract that I've just signed. Would there be a chance of getting the cheque to me quick as poss cause I'm away on holidays come the 16th. Two weeks on a Youth Med package at a big resort, any chance yous could get the money to me quick would be good as it would pretty much do for spending money.

I do look forward to meeting in London.

Morvern Callar

I used the goldish lighter on a Silk Cut as I re-read the

letter then I signed it, re-read it, put it in an envelope and licked the flap.

I'd to be up 05.30 to start 07.00 at the superstore so I put the CD of This Is How It Feels by The Golden Palominos on and got ready for my bed.

I fell asleep when Track 6 was playing though it just might have been 7.

As PER usual when taking the train from the port, the driver took me up the front cab with him. Like I was a mascot. It was Red Hanna on the 12.25 who carried my bag up the engine. In the noisy cab we climbed behind The Complex east towards the Back Settlement with Beinn Mheadhonach in the distance. We moved west through the pass, the Falls platform above The Turbines Bar and towards the village beyond the power station. Branches hung out towards my side-window then swished back as we passed. When we rounded the corner beside the shore-line with my fosterdad looking straight ahead, I stepped over behind him, looking out and up through the window in the cab door. The railwayline straightened and you saw the top of the stairs, the hotel with the pointing-up tower, then towards the graveyard as we moved along you saw the pines where the flowering Tree Church would be.

At the crossing loop Red Hanna carried my bag back to a coach. He kissed me on the cheek and tried to give me a twenty but I wouldnt let him.

After the run down to The Central Belt the train came into the big station. When I got out and turned round you saw Lanna step from the last coach with her ghetto blaster and bag. I got a taxi.

The taxi did 85 on the motorway and you saw a good deal new signs from The Highway Code.

Inside the terminal building the flight number was up on the telly-display thing: six and a half hour delay. You gave your bag to the check-in person and they let you choose a seat from an actual model of the aeroplane. I chose a no-smoker over the wing so I wouldnt be near Lanna. The check-in person put a sticker on my boarding card then gave me these vouchers cause of delay.

I took the escalators up to The Aerogrill Bar. Lanna was at the far end with the ghetto-blaster at her feet. I turned and moved back downstairs where there was another bar called The Flight Deck so I plumped for that. There was a Formula One machine so's I waited till the kid got off it then I rested my Southern Comfort and lemonade on top the machine and played away. I could never get onto the best level so I let out a big huff of disappointedness and looked round. I walked over and sat at the bar. I've been delayed by six and a half hours; I'll be here all night and I'll no be there till about ten in the morning, I says to the barmaid.

You'd be better through the Departure Lounge before they close the Duty Free; theyve got a good bar there too, the barmaid goes.

Aye? I went.

I had another Southern Comfort and lemonade then I picked up my shoulder bag and walked to the Departure Lounge.

The security girl explained I couldnt go out again but I told her that was okay. The metal detector beeped when I walked under it. I mustve been mortal cause I sumley supposed it was the glitter in my knee.

The security girl patted me down across the shoulders then round to the front of the dress her fingers fluttering over the bra but she touched the wee plastic container round my neck.

Whats in that? she says.

Oh thats for when you go swimming so you can take any keys or money with you and not have to leave them on the beach, I went.

Anything in it?

My flat keys, I says.

That'll be it. Can you go through again without them? she went.

I lifted the luminous string over my head and handed it to her then walked back through. The machine didnt beep. The security girl kneeled and touched me just where the skirt started then pushed both hands round and up across my bum pressing the dress material against me. She jumped up and goes, Right thanks, then handed the keys back. My shoulder bag had gone through this conveyor belt thing so I grabbed it and moved off to the Duty Free shop.

Standing in one of the brightly lit aisles I double-checked my spending money got from that novel. I had £350 cash changed and a envelope of traveller's cheques: £2,000 worth.

I bought a carton of Silk Cut, a bottle Southern Comfort and a waterproof watch. I paid with a £200 traveller's cheque. Smiling I walked over to the bar.

Can I have a Chaos please?

What?

A Chaos, Southern Comfort mixed with Baileys; thats what we call it, I says.

Aye? went the barman and he laughed.

A guy at the end of the bar in a T-shirt who had been yapping to the barman laughed too.

I drank the Chaos then ordered another.

Want a drink? I says to the guy in the T-shirt.

We had a bit of a ceilidh and I bought the guy a few more pints lager. He was quite funny with his Central Belt accent.

Let's sit over there, I says when he bought a round. We sat on this long purplish bench where Lanna would be able to see us when she came in.

I was nodding at him as he told a story about a night out. He told about his local pub. Everyone was so poor that you only dare hand over pound notes across the bar cause if you showed even a fiver you'd get hassle all night. You could go in and spend £40 if it was in pound notes but woe betide if you had a tenner. I leaned over a little and started the snogging of him. He put his arms round me and after a bit I gave him seven out of ten on the snogging front.

Is there anywhere we can have a little lie down? Just a bit of a cuddle cause I'm jiggered and this flight's not going till about half six, I says.

A lie down? he goes.

Aye.

Youre something else you, he says and laughs.

He put his arm round me and sort of tickled my nose with the fringe of his hair. I moved my head back a bit.

Nah, I've really got to get going, he says.

Eh? I goes.

I've got to get away home, I'm this shift the morrow.

What do you mean; I thought you were away on this flight? I says.

What? I work here. I drive the polishing machine up and down all those lousy corridors.

God almighty, I went and shook my head.

He stood up and ruffled my hair, Have a good time there, and take care, he says and he stood up and walked over by the bar. He nodded and winked at the barman then marched out.

I looked one way then the other. The Departure Lounge had really filled up. Just then Lanna walked in. Two guys with taches were walking either side her. She pretended not to see. She sat down way over by the Duty Free.

I leaned forward and took out the bottle Southern Comfort. On the plastic Duty Free carrier bag was written:

I twisted open the top of the Southern Comfort and poured it into my glass.

I was lying on the bench with my legs curled up and I'd tugged the thin dress down over as much of my legs as I could cause it was cold. Someone was shoogling me. I opened eyes. Everyone was moving. I sat up and used the lighter on a Silk Cut. Lanna was sat over with the two boys who were draining some cans of beer. The flight had been called. I squinted at my watch: half six. I picked up the shoulder bag. All the seats and floor were littered with empty cans and bottles. I followed the crowd down a long corridor then onto this banister and floor that moved. At the gate a rubber tube took you into the front door of the plane.

The stewardess moved her mouth at me and pointed to my ear.

I switched off the Walkman. Me and this bother boy behind me had to remove our Walkmans till after take off cause the music can get picked up on the captain's headphones.

Hey, this is good stuff, I bet he'd like it, goes the bother boy, laughing.

I moved along the aisle to the no-smoker seats over the wing. Lanna was sat directly across from my seat with another guy next her. She mustve chosen that to try and get away from me. Our eyes met and I almost started laughing. The bother boy with the Walkman was sat next me. I started putting my seat belt on and straight away the bother boy says, What tapes have you got?

I looked round but no drinks were getting served. Next thing the plane was bumping along then swinging round onto the bright, lit-up runway. I keeked over at the young guy sat beside Lanna. The plane started shaking like nobody's business then trundling down the runway. I could feel sweat in my palm and you didnt have Lanna there to hold hands. Lanna was snogging the guy next her and we werent even off the ground. I says to the bother boy, What resort are you going to? He says the name of a place.

Right, I goes and I grabbed his hand and held on.

There were bad sinking feelings. Clouds were through the window next to my cheek. A stewardess was pushing a drinks trolley downhill on the aisle.

What you drinking then? I says to the bother boy but when I turned round he'd gone fast asleep still holding my hand. I ordered three Southern Comforts and lemonade and a can of beer in case the bother boy woke up.

The ice cubes in the plastic cup vibrated so I did the last drink in a oner. The Southern Comforts came in tiny wee bottles. I drank the can of beer too then stepped over the sleeping boy.

Lanna was still in a clinch with seat 27B.

I paid a visit to the toilet then hung round outside smoking a Silk Cut. They had started serving a meal.

Back in the seat he didnt wake up so I ate all my meal with another can of beer then I ate the sweet and cheese out of the bother boy's tray. When all the trays were cleared away I says no to coffee. There was a leaflet in the seat back; it showed stretching exercises for long flights. I laughed then nodded off for a bit.

When I woke my ears ached. The plane was coming in.

You saw no greenish hills. There was only the brownish-ness of rocky places then a dry-looking reservoir with layers of whiteish salt. Then you saw nothing but houses that were the colour white and the bright blue of rec-tangle-shaped swimming pools. Dots of layed-out fruit trees moved under the wing and we crossed a road with tiny cars then you could see all this dry sticky-up grass as we came over a tall perimeter fence and concrete streaked with rubber rose up towards then with a bang the plane landed and everyone clapped and cheered. The bother boy sat bolt upright, bleary eyed; he just started clapping too.

Coming out the plane into the morning it was already hot like there was a hair dryer in your face. Lanna had gone well ahead and got on the first bus to the terminal. I got on the next. The bus had no seats; all stood close to each other, sweating and their arms held up gripping straps on the roof. All swayed as the bus moved off.

In the airport building it was cooler with the air con-ditioning. You walked past a booth with passport men inside wearing uniforms that were the colour green. I held up my passport but they just winked at me. You could smell their foreign-smell cigarettes; I wanted to buy a packet straight away.

Lanna was across at the far side of the conveyor belt. I lit a Silk Cut and walked to the toilet. I splashed my face and used some spray-on deodorant.

When I got back, my bag was one of the first to come round. I yanked it up and walked away. Lanna was still stood waiting. I passed the customs bench and out the sliding door. There was a long railing with people leaning along it holding out cards with names on them. At the end of the railing there was a big sign:

YOUTH MED TOURS

HOTEL ROZINANTE BUS.

There were gangs of young folk with ghetto-blasters standing in groups talking and laughing. I carried my bag out the front doors into the heat.

The taxi at the top of the queue had an older man in. The older man got out and smiled. He put my bag in the boot. When I shut the back door the skin on my legs stuck to the hot seat. I edged forward so I could sit on the dress material and I started winding the window down. The driver climbed in the front left side.

I says the resort and Hotel Rozinante.

He moved the gear stick that was fixed to the steering column. It was an old Mercedes Benz. I'd never been in a Mercedes Benz before.

Breeze came in the window as the taxi moved out the airport. You saw the clear greeny blades of a palm tree standing high in the bright light. We were on a straight towards the sea. The lines on the roads were the colour yellow. The No Overtaking sign had the red car on the left. My skin felt queer and sure enough there was a kind of film of dust on everything.

We came to a town, a port but with big, all different yachts along the front.

Hey, I goes and I made the sign to raise a glass to your lips.

The taxi driver started saying words. I kept making the sign and he pointed to the meter. I shrugged. He drove up and down streets for a while till he found parking. I was smiling in the back. I got out but he stayed sat there. I shook my head and smiled, waving for him to come. He laughed and climbed out locking the car. He says some of his words and I followed him to the waterfront. There was a bar called Delfin and there was the shape of a dolphin outside. There was a long dark bar.

One beer and . . .? I goes.

The taxi driver says something in his words. It was a liqueur and the barman put saucers of olives and things in front us. I paid and held the beer up to the taxi driver.

Slainte, I goes and he says his word.

With the change I crossed to the cigarette machine and got a pack of Ducados.

I offered one to the taxi driver and lit it for him with

the goldish lighter. He talked with the barman who leaned on a dishtowel that covered the beer tap with the big eagle on it. Their own words were all you heard and they never even looked at me except when saying thank you in their words when I gave money for another small beer or offered round a Ducados. They became quiet when some football came on the big telly then they talked more. I wasnt even listening to the sounds of the words as I leaned on the bar.

Eventually I jumped off the stool and walked to the toilet. As we left, the barman waved. I followed the taxi driver to the street where we were parked and he opened the door for me. It was stifling inside.

As we drove out of the town you could see flats like The Complex, just as shabby with all different blinds and curtains. Further up the coast things changed. There were new villas all painted white, built out of every rock above the sea. Some were really big with satellite dishes and sprinkler systems for the garden. The coast was like this right up to a few miles from the resort when the villas stopped.

I says out loud, Lucky so and so's; such a lot of happiness in one place.

The taxi driver dropped me at the Hotel Rozinante. I gave him a tip that was half the fare. He tried to give some back but I shook my head and crossed the road gazing up at the height of the hotel. In the foyer this courier type came up.

I'm with Youth Med, I says.

Oh, are the buses here? he says.

I got a lift.

A lift? You cant get a lift. Theres an official bus for you, he says.

Can I have my room key?

Whats your name?

Morvern Callar.

How do you spell that? he says walking round the reception front.

C-a-l-l-a-r, I goes.

Callar, he went and he looked over at me then says, Morvern, more quiet.

Aye, I went.

Thats a local word. Are you from here? he says.

Nut, I goes.

Youre in 1169 on the eleventh floor with a Miss Phimister, he says and handed over the keys.

Right, I went.

Sorry about the delay on your flight over here, out Youth Med's control of course. Now theres a friendly get together in the function room tonight with a free glass of bubbly for everyone. So we can all get to know one another better for the two weeks to come. Theres games at the swimming pool tomorrow morning, what we like to think of as an icebreaker. He did this laugh then says, And we all go to Aqualand the next day. Your evenings are of course your own, at the moment, though we'll have a disco on Friday.

Right, I says and walked away then I stopped and turned.

Lift is straight ahead, he goes.

What does callar mean? I went.

Callar? he goes, looking up from the list, then he says, callar, ah, it means, ah, silence, to say nothing, maybe. He stared at me.

I turned and walked on then took the lift to the eleventh floor.

I put my bag in the wardrobe and kept all my money safely on me. I sat on one of the beds with my face in my hands. Then I stood and took the lift down. I left the key at reception then walked out the hotel. I looked left then right, started walking to the left then turned the other way. I stopped, stamped one foot and walked on.

Down on the long esplanade I stepped in the first restaurant. I sat at a table that faced out to sea. Every bit sand was covered in people. I watched the bodies get carried up on the winch till they fell to the water.

There were no words in the menu just colour photographs of the food and a number that was the price. I pointed to the photo of the omelette with the blueish background, the photo of bread with a greenish background and the photo of a Pepsi with a yellowy background. The girl walked away after writing things down on a pad.

The girl put the food down on the paper table cloth and thousands were fives so I handed her two. She turned and walked away. I ate and drank quick. Soon folk were starting to come up off the beach. The girl brought back change in a saucer. I stood up, lifted all the notes and put them in my purse then walked down from the restaurant and on up the line. There was a bar called The Asparagus so I walked straight in and asked for a Southern Comfort with lemonade. I sat on a stool near the open air.

I had on the mirrored shades and I was sure a group of drinkers were staring at me but studying the two boys and two girls you realised they just had that look where they were trying to focus on things in front and it seemed they were watching everything.

They all looked about my age but the guys mustve been in motorcycle accidents; they had plasters and gauze stuck all over their arms.

One of the girls came up to the bar and ordered four pints of water. She turned to me and says, Want to buy anything love, E's, blow?

I took off the shades and goes, Nut.

We're out our faces, she goes and giggled.

Aye? I went.

Come and join us; whats your name? I'm Andrea.

I smiled and says, Morvern.

I walked over and sat with them, Andrea goes, Hey, eh, everyone this is Morvern. The guys were all really red raw with sunburn.

Hiya Morvern, went the reddest, pleased to meet you,

I'm Trevor, this is Lucy and Andrea and the monkey over there is Dazzer.

Whats happened to yous? I goes.

He won the competition with Darren here, says Lucy.

Sunburn competition on our first day here, marvellous fun it was, went Trevor.

Started just with oil, then we nicked olive oil off the cafe tables, says Dazzer.

Then a bit of silver foil on my arm here, went Trevor, flipping up the gauze so's you could see a patch of blood with poison under.

Oooh ya, I goes.

I did that too, says Dazzer.

Yeah but I bettered it: the lens of some old sod's glasses, went Trevor, sticking out his leg and lifting another gauze where there was just a wee black hole right into his leg.

What about that with the stitches in it? I goes.

They all laughed.

We've been here six nights and I've been up at casualty three running; we get these at The Waterloo, says Trevor.

Dazzer goes, We spent nearly all our money on drugs the first night here so we go up The Waterloo for free beer in the evenings to economise in these difficult times.

Come along, it's a scream, went Andrea.

Okey-dokey, I goes.

Drink up folks. Waterloo, says Trevor.

Dazzer goes, Not a chance mate, I'm going to get to

the supermarket for some bog roll; this is the third bar we've been to with none.

None in The Waterloo anyway, shouted Lucy and they all started laughing.

Nah, nah, but I'll go to that supermarket place by the point and just buy the stuff with money then I'm away to the hotel to sit on the throne, I can feel an Atlantic cable coming on, says Dazzer.

Get us some as well, that bitch of a maid wont give us any more; I was well taken short this morning, went Lucy.

Trevor turned to me and says, Every night after the raves we chuck the bog rolls over the balcony and let them all roll down the front of the building then everyone in the opposite tower block does it too; looks bloody marvellous it does, these long streamers all down the front of the hotel.

Makes you proud, Dazzer slowly nodded.

Cmon darling, Andrea there'll look after you; we'll show you a sight to remember.

We all moved out The Asparagus Bar. Dazzer knocked over an empty glass that shattered, Sorry, he shouted back.

Trevor goes, You see love, we cannot swim, we cannot sunbathe, so with all due respect, we drink. He started laughing and then a coughing fit was all you heard.

Hey, Dazzer, whats the word for bog paper? goes Andrea.

I know that, says Dazzer. We walked in the supermarket. There were three young girls on the check-out tills. Dazzer marched up to them and began a mime of what you did with toilet paper, Any bog roll darling, y'know, uh, uh.

It was getting very late in The Waterloo. Dazzer had gone to their hotel with the toilet paper and I was mortal as a newt.

Another lad walked up to the bar. We all turned round.

Two free pints please, the lad says. A small crowd wandered over to watch. The lad put his arm on the bar. The barman took one saw out a sterilised bucket. Right, half a pint, the barman goes and he drew the saw on its own weight over the lad's arm. A pint, went the barman as he pushed the saw forward. You saw the white scratches on the tanned skin. The barman says, A pint and a half, two pints. You could see the last pull scraped the skin open. A few folk cheered.

Two pints bollocks, goes Trevor standing up.

No. Look, I'll buy another round, I went.

When I carried the drinks back Andrea had fallen asleep on the long seat.

Dazzer came stumbling through the doorway with a bunch of guys.

How are you doing? I waved.

Hey, whats happening. Some set up eh? Dazzer says.

This is sheer mental, they'll all get Aids, I goes.

I'm pie in the sky love, went Dazzer slumping onto the long seat and just sitting on Andrea's hair. He says, I met these lads I know from the football and they bought me about ten pints of Guinness. Look at the state of this crew; how come a beautiful chick like you is running with us, where are your friends and that, you shouldnt be hanging around alone.

I'm not a chick, I goes.

Yeah, well you know, it's kind of strange.

I'm sharing the hotel room with my best friend but we've fallen out. You wont believe this but I've just come across Europe on the same flight without even sitting beside her. You wouldnt believe it, I went.

Dazzer sat up, Try me, he goes.

I told Dazzer the story of our fall-out, just saying it was cause she bumped my ex. As I spoke Dazzer nodded his baldy head but it got closer and closer to the table so I was hurrying the last bit about leaving my case in the room and the key at reception. When I finished I says, I'm a bit worried about her.

Amazing. Amazing world. I was standing in The Victory, four pubs down, just before I came here. Theres a drunken little babe with your accent told me the exact same story, slurred Dazzer and his cheek touched the table.

What? I goes and stood up. Suddenly there was this smell. It was Dazzer. All that Guinness and he should have gone to the toilet.

It's Trevor again, shouted the barman, How many pints Trev? and folk were crowding round.

Eight pints, sixteen strokes then get me the ambulance for casualty when I've finished the last one, says Trevor.

Up came the saw and down went Trevor's arm on the bar.

Not on my tattoos, was the last thing I heard Trevor say then I belted out the door and down to The Victory.

Lanna was leaning against a guy and the same two with taches from back in The Aerogrill Bar were plagueing her. I walked straight up and she smiled, pushed forward then fell against me. I gave her a big hug and all the males looked at us. I pulled her outside by the hand. We stumbled along together.

It was a very hot night. We were swaying under a tall streetlight while I tried to work out what way with insects whizzing round and round the filament above us and there was a real noise of castanets: it was the crickets buzzing in every bush. We were lost but we walked on and when we swayed we just started having the hysterics.

At long last we came to the water but you couldnt tell what end of the beach you were at. You could hear the water way out on the point but there were no streetlights out there.

We started walking out onto the point so we could get to the sand by the sea and have a lie down. We climbed under some sort of string then we were stumbling about on the sand till I heard the water right in front of us. We sat down breathing heavy. The sand felt all queer under me. The ground started shaking and pale lights were in the surf. I stood up then I turned round and saw bright lights coming towards us and you heard deep, big powerful engines motoring hard. Shadows twisted round us. A massive dumper truck drove towards us then pulled away to the left. Lanna got up and we started running but it was difficult. We were running on plastic bags and newspapers and tin cans. It was a rubbish dump they were filling in and reclaiming from the sea. The dump truck tipped out sand and a digger began spreading it. They were building a beach during the night.

We clambered down to the road then we began walking towards the tallest buildings.

The night porter wouldnt let us in the front door of the hotel. Right enough our legs were covered in a sort of red muck. He made us come in the kitchen entrance and while we were walking among all the ovens and stainless steel Lanna lifted up a flan case and put it up the side of her shirt then round under her jerkin.

The bar was open so without asking me Lanna walked up and bought two pints lager. We just sat staring at them then Lanna stood up. I led the way to the lift. We got out on the first floor cause someone had been sick in it. It took a long time to climb the stairs. I kept hearing liquid splashing and when I turned to look you saw Lanna had put the pints of lager in the jerkin pockets and it was sloshing everywhere.

We got in the room and Lanna collapsed on a bed. Without saying a word to me she fell fast asleep. I took the pint glasses out the pockets and pulled the flan case from under the blouse. I stripped her and brushed all the crumbs off the bed. I tried not to look at her body.

I shuffled out on the balcony cause I wasnt going to get to sleep. You were sure you could see things moving out in the darkness beyond the balcony edge. Sure enough, streamers of toilet paper were dangling down the fronts of the skyscrapers but also every so often the plastic toilet brushes and the cylinders holding them were floating slowly down to the streetlights below. You heard a distant cheering.

I moved back in to the bathroom where I stripped and had an ice-cold freezing shower. I used a towel on me and put on the clean orangey dress from out my bag. I left my hair wet and put my money in under the bag.

I sat out on the balcony again then after a while I heard it. I leaned out a little on the balcony and it was coming from one of the rooms under us. It was greeting. A grown man greeting. I pushed the wet hair back from my forehead.

I sneaked along the corridor. It was easy to hear what room it was coming from:

1022

I tapped my knuckles on the door. The guy came straight up and opened it: my age but shorter, his face was red with the greeting. He looked right at me.

Are you all right? I says.

He walked back in the room leaving the door open. I pushed the door wide then edged in. He was sitting on the end of the bed by the telephone. It was a single room. He had smooth-looking skin.

My mother has died. It took me a year to save for this holiday and my brother just phoned to tell me she died, he says in a Central Belt accent.

I was standing at the corner of the corridor. I saw that the door behind me was still open though in hotels it's law they shut. The door springs would have been removed cause bound in parcel tape they make good weapons for the boys.

Will you have to go back? I goes.

Funeral, he went.

I slid down the wall so the backs of my thighs were on the cool polished stone of the floor. I sat there at right angles to the bed.

It's good of you to be concerned, he says.

I'm pretty wasted; cant sleep, I went.

He nodded then sobbed wiping away at his nose.

Listen, I'll tell you about my fostermother's funeral, I says and I started speaking.

I sat cross-legged in front then I straightened and held my face up to the ceiling; my dried hair had fallen forward over both my shoulders onto his hairless-feeling thighs but when it hung down the middle of my back it felt warm straight away under its thicknesses. I reached down between my legs to move his fingers correctly and I was just saturated there. I'd kept the movements going then devoured it all in quick gulps with my head held back then I leaned down on him again so my hair fell forward over one shoulder and the back felt cool again. He was breathing quick.

When he was on top he moved too efficiently, there was no going beyond; you knew it was too athletic to be really rampant but he was an eight out of ten snogger. Still, I clung to him for grim life.

After, he touched each and says, Nice hair, nice nose, nice lips, nice skin, nice *girl*.

Thanks, I goes.

Nothing else went on. He was one of those guys the tide went out on after two goes.

I woke. Something wet, maybe bleeding, was by my hand. I sat up; it was the guy's used flunky. I put my feet down on the coolness of stone. Holding the rubber between fingers I walked onto the balcony. I held it up to my face then swung my arm out and flung the rubber into the night sky. It sparkled for split seconds and some separated then it slowly floated down into the darkness.

I breathed in air and the model city was glorious as anything. It was very still, the cooling towers of the high rises had cherry-coloured beacons on top and all the lights seemed to be a wee bit different in colour. It was all so beautiful I grabbed the railing. I sat back in the plastic chair and saw dawn come over the sea. During the night they had finished the new beach and far out on the point you could see the raked sand appear out the dark and as it got lighter some people were going down on it to claim a patch.

The door to 1022 could only be locked from the inside so I pulled it behind me and quietly pitter-pattered in my bare feet up our room.

Where on earth have you been? Lanna sat up.

I smiled and shrugged.

Lanna says, Youve been with a guy on your first night here, havent you Morvy? I'm jealous, she laughed and started kicking out under the single sheet covering her.

Cmon lets Immac our bikini lines and get down there, Lanna says.

Everyone was in swimsuits howling, Here we go here we go here we go, in the dining room of the Hotel Rozinante. There was a big bench littered with cornflakes and spilt milk. I got a bowl and piled in as much sugar as cereal.

Lanna and me walked over to a table then saw why it was free. There was a large splatter of sick beside it. We sat at the end of a table where these guys started whistling at us.

Let's go, Lanna says.

We sat down by the swimming pool where all the male couriers were smoking, wearing sunglasses and counting out money. You didnt get a minute's peace alone with your hangover and the entire population of the dining room trooped down the crazy paving to the pool led by a beefy courier with a megaphone.

RIGHT, ALL GIRLS ON ONE SIDE OF THE POOL AND ALL BLOKES ON THE OTHER.

Lanna and me tried to ignore him but since it was only Youth Med youngsters round the pool it wasnt easy to blend in with other holidaymakers so we sauntered over to stand in line with the other young lassies in bikinis and swimsuits like us. Over the blueish water trembling from the swimming pool pump we faced the line of pale hung-over men. The guy from 1022 wasnt there.

RIGHT THEN. LET'S GET TO KNOW ONE ANOTHER *A LITTLE BIT BETTER* THEN. NO SPOILSPORTS NOW CAUSE THIS IS YOUR REAL HANGOVER CURE, LADIES AND GENTLEMEN. The courier held up a large jet-black canvas sack.

THE RULES OF THE GETTING-IN-THE-SACK-GAME ARE QUITE SIMPLE AND PERFECTLY FAIR. YOU'LL NOTICE WE HAVE A FINE SUPPLY OF THESE BAGS. I'M GONNA PICK OUT A LAD AND A LOVELY LADY AND ASK THEM TO DO A LIL DEMONSTRATION FOR US BUT BEFORE WE DO LET ME ADDRESS A SPECIAL WORD TO ALL YOU LOVELY LADIES OVER THERE WHO HAPPEN TO BE WEARING BIKINIS NOT SWIM-SUITS. EVERY FORTNIGHT WE GET LOVELY LADIES BEING UNFAIR TO THEIR COLLEAGUES IN SWIMSUITS. IT'S VERY MUCH AGAINST THE

SPIRIT OF THE FUN SO PLEASE DO AS YOU ARE TOLD OR WE'LL INVOLVE YOU IN OUR LITTLE CONTEST LATER FOR SPOILSPORTS IN BIKINIS. CAN WE HAVE OUR VOLUNTEERS PLEASE. YOU AND YOU.

Everyone laughed as the couple walked over.

IN YOU GET.

The couple climbed into the big black sack together.

NOW YOU'LL HAVE NOTICED THAT THE LOVELY LADY IN THE GREEN BIKINI IS IN THE SACK WITH THE GENTLEMAN IN THE RED TRUNKS. I'LL JUST TIE THE TOP HERE. NOW, ARE YOU OKAY IN THERE?

There were muffled sounds and everyone around the pool except me laughed.

NOW I'M ONLY GOING TO THROW OUR LITTLE CATS IN THE BAG HERE INTO THE SWIMMING POOL IF THEY DONT GET INTO THE SPIRIT OF THINGS. SO. CAN YOU TWO IN THERE PLEASE NOW **SWAP YOUR SWIMSUITS!**

There was laughing all round the pool and people started looking at each other. Me and Lanna were wearing bikinis.

NOTHING TO BE SHY ABOUT LADIES. IT'S GREAT FOR YOUR SUNTAN. RIGHT YOU TWO, OUT YOU COME.

The courier untied the sack and the couple inside stood up. Everyone started laughing louder, especially from the boy's side. The couriers sat up on the diving board smiled and smoked.

The couple stood with the sack round their feet, the girl's bare bosom seemed awful white in the bright sun and she was holding up the big baggy trunks with both hands; the underneath of the boy's chin was glowing from the bright bikini top that was flopped emptily round his chest hairs.

People were whistling and shouting. I says, What a utter total nightmare.

Cmon Morvern it'll be a laugh; I'm no shy, I'm going topless on the beach anyways, I just hope I get a real honeybunch not some grot, says Lanna.

THATS WHAT I CALL A SPORTING GIRL. NOW TWO LENGTHS OF THE POOL PLEASE.

The couple splashed in the pool and started swimming along. The lassie had to windmill one arm round and round so's she could hold the trunks on with the other. The fabric of the bikini bottom had tugged up the guy's behind.

A courier shadowed them along the edge filming with a camcorder.

RIGHT. NEXT COUPLE PLEASE. YOU AND YOU.

I glanced left then right but the courier was pointing at me. I walked round the edge of the pool.

CMON NOW. THE VIDEO OF THIS EVENT WILL BE AVAILABLE IN THE FOYER TONIGHT FOR £5.99.

I climbed into the sack with a guy who stepped in. The black material was pulled up to our shoulders by two couriers. We both sat down then the top of the sack was gathered up and tied. There was total blackness. Outside the sack you heard screams and splashes.

Eh, nice to meet you, went the voice in the darkness.

Hello, I goes.

Whats your name then? says the voice.

Morvern, I goes.

Suppose we'd better get on with it, eh? the voice went.

I sighed and started worming my way out of my bikini bottoms.

READY YET? came from next to us and my body jumped.

Just a minute, says the voice.

YOU'D BETTER BE OUT IN TEN SECONDS OR IT'S IN THE POOL WITH YA.

Is that not called murder? I whispered.

Quick. Hurry up, the voice goes and the material of his trunks was pushed in my face.

You heard him forcing his leg out and pulling on my bikini bottoms. Are you taking your top off? the voice asked.

I stretched round undoing it then held it out. It got taken away.

Hey it wont reach round, the voice went.

Come here, I says and reached over. I tried to tie it round his chest but he was too broad.

RIGHT ARE YOU TWO PERFORMING IN THERE

OR WHAT, PLENTY OF TIME FOR THAT ON
YOUR RETURN TRIP.

You'll need to tie it round your neck, I goes.

Nah, I'll tie it round my forehead, a bandanna.

I was tugging on the big trunks but when I tried to
tighten them with the cord it pulled right out the lining.

Then the light was dazzling and hurt my eyes. I stood
quickly holding up the trunks. There was movement and
coloured clothes everywhere. I squinted at people staring
and a video camera waving right up at me; I put my hand
up to my bosoms. I looked down at my bikini bottoms
all stretched on him so you could see everything.

RIGHT, IN THE POOL.

There was just an enormous push so I hit the water
with my mouth still open then the guy in my bikini landed
on top me. I doggy-paddled up the top end of the pool
then when I paddled back I saw my sodden bikini top
round the forehead of the guy I was in the sack with.

We've to get back in, he smiled.

I cooried so's my topmost bits were under the surface
but you could see his eyes being able to make them out
in the shallowy water.

Morvy, someone shouted. My head yanked up but it
was just Lanna, bare-breasted with boy's trunks on that
she quite suited. She waved, ducked down and got tied
up in a sack with some boy.

RIGHT OUT YOU COME AND IN HERE.

I pushed myself up with one hand and held the trunks
with the other but I couldnt manage so reached up and

the guy with my bikini on took my hand and pulled me out.

Water poured off me. There were about fifteen closed sacks in front of us, each of them moving slowly with no sounds coming out. Me and the guy were tied back in to the blackness.

This is like living hell on earth, I says into the darkness. We were both breathing heavily in the wetness and the chlorine smells. We started peeling off our stuff. He squeezed out my bikini and you could feel the wet warm patch. Then he just held me under the arm with his hands. He tried to kiss me but in the dark I turned my head aside. His nose nuzzled around my wet hair then he whispered if I would do something.

I told him where to go.

Oh, come on, in for a penny, trapped in here with a naked woman is getting to me a little, he says and laughed.

Do it yourself, I says.

I will if you wont, he goes and you heard his movements begin.

I tried to twist round on my side so I could give him a long kick but his weight was sitting on most of the sacking so it was impossible to stretch out.

His quick, mad and desperate-sounding movements went on. I kept still then he gasped in the darkness.

I tried to stand up but the tied top pulled me down onto him and he put his arms round me then laughed. We rolled over together then I shouted, Youre crazy we'll go in the water and drown.

Something kicked against us and he let me go. I finished tying the bikini top on then I wormed back into the bottoms. There was a tug and the smell of outside came in.

I NOW PRONOUNCE YOU MAN AND WIFE the courier shouted through his loud-hailer. I dived in the pool and swam across it. When I climbed out the other side I looked back over and saw that Lanna was still inside her sack by the diving board. There was no movement you could see.

A line of girls who hadnt taken their bikini tops off during the changing were under guard on the other side of the diving board. The courier with the camcorder was dancing in among them filming close-ups.

NOW THESE CULPRITS ARE GUILTY OF NOT REMOVING BIKINI TOPS SO THEY ARE NOW PART OF OUR LITTLE TALENT CONTEST FOR LADIES ONLY HERE. BRING ON THE TORTURE DEVICE.

Parading down the crazy paving, a courier was carrying a big square of chamois leather. The beefy courier took out a stop watch and stood beside the first girl while the chamois leather was brought through the crowd. The chamois was folded aside to show a massive block of dripping blueish-coloured ice.

NOW LADIES AND GENTLEMEN WE APPLY THE CHUNK OF ICE AND I TIME THE SPEED TO FULL ERECTION ON EACH LOVELY LADY AND THE MOST SENSITIVE NIPPLE ON ALL THESE

BREASTS WILL BE DECLARED WINNER OF THE
NIPPLE ERECTION CONTEST. ITS OWNER WILL
WIN THE PRIZE: A ROMANTIC CANDLE-LIT
DINNER WITH ME. APPLY THE ICE.

I shook my head and turned away. I started running up
the crazy paving and took the lift to the tenth floor. I
pushed the door to 1022 aside. The bed was made and his
case was gone. In the wet bikini I lay down on the bed.

So much sweat was pouring down the dead décolleté top
I'd on you'd have been as well taking it off. I stood still
and took a glug out my two-litre water bottle. Lanna and
the two raver boys had worked themselves ov੭ to the
bridge from the floor on the chill-out area. The DJ had
taken us right into the hardest 'core and you could see he
was letting it run more Ambient for a while before he'd
start building up the energy again. You didnt want to get
taken on that round the whole way again so I looked at
my fingers for a bit with the light swishing off them and
the reflections off the retina coming back when you turned
your head across the lasers.

I'm jiggered, I says to Lanna and walked out over the
bridge. Lanna and the guy just in shorts and a ski hat
followed, then the other lad with the gone-eyes.

I'm roasting, I goes and poured some of the bottle over
my hair.

How are you feeling? went Lanna.

Quite posey, I says leaning back and shaking my wet hair.

Yes honey and youre looking so good too, goes Lanna.

I gritted my teeth and looked at the twitchy boys.

So whats the scene down the coast then? says Lanna to the one with the hat.

Up, up the coast but it's in all the little places. Much more relaxed, ambient, cushions, smoking not Es. It's DJs coming down from the north, from the cold countries. Music you can shake hair to or just calm to and the girls take their clothes off as well; all due respect and that but a girl'll just come up to you and start ramming her tongue down your throat. No hassles or anything, just to hell with fire regulations, they switch off all the lights just have the music going and if youre into it, a gang on the floor squirming about.

Total love-ins man, the other guy says.

Yeah, the rave scene here is just evolving on to the next thing like a disease that adapts.

Let's go to Reverberation, went the other guy.

The guy with the hat says, The Reverb is open twenty-four hours, two arenas, they just close one and clean the other. Our mate Shashy came here for a week at Easter and a month later he was found in The Reverb; he'd just been living there on burgers and orange juice.

Lanna was in stitches at this.

I'm away back the hotel, I goes.

Not think theyre cute? Lanna whispered in my ear.

I gave her a look.

Dont get weird on me, Lanna goes.

Are you going to ask one back? I says.

Both. If only one comes we can do a duet on him, goes Lanna and she put her head back to laugh.

I might go on somewhere else, I went.

Well dont forget we're going to Aqualand at eleven, Lanna says.

I'll see you, I goes and handed her the water bottle.

Hoi, push the beds together and keep them warm, Lanna shouted.

I nodded to the bouncer guys and walked down the wide street towards the hotel wiping sweat beads away then you felt the heat drying it on you.

Up a side street was a tall palm tree and there mustve been a cicada in it cause that loud electric drill sound they make was coming from the leaves. A guy with no shirt was on a balcony screaming, Shut up, you drive me mad. He lobbed an empty beer bottle at the tree and it tumbled through the leaves then smashed on the concrete of a flowerbed wall.

Further on a group of guys were working busily at some baby palm trees in the central reservation. You supposed they were municipal workers at first then you noticed the shiny tops and sunglasses. They were carefully ripping out the trees then flinging them across the tarmac. One of them shouted at me, Hey, beautiful, fancy going halfers on a bastard?

I rung the buzzer and the night porter let me in. Up in Lanna and I's room I took a shower with my sunglasses on. I used talc here and there then brushed my teeth. The room stunk of the industrial-strength cockroach repellent that Lanna always used. I lay on the bed then sat forward on the end with face in hands. I lay back again then started greeting and dead quickly just stopped. I stood up and got dressed. I rode down in the lift and left our room key with the night porter at reception. He watched me with a look when I turned and took the stairs. I climbed really slowly and stopped on the fifth for a breather.

I sneaked along the corridor and opened 1022. I put on the light then when I saw the coast was clear I locked the door behind and lay on the bed where I mustve fallen straight asleep.

Heat of another perfect day was starting and in the distance you could here the chattering of drills on the roads. I climbed up to our room and knocked on the door.

Whos there? came Lanna's voice.

Me, I goes.

The door opened a little and Lanna looked out. Under her eyes was black.

What time is it? she says opening the door wide.

It's half nine. Thought you wanted to go to Aqualand, I went and walked in.

We've taken more E, she says.

Hi, I nodded to the guy in the bed; the one with the gone-eyes.

Yes, hi, want one? he goes pointing to the dresser.

Nah, I went, reaching in and getting my bag out.

Where'd you go last night then? Lanna says.

I shrugged.

Where are you going with the bag?

I'm taking it to reception if youre going to have people trekking in and out here every night.

Excuse us, Lanna says and took me by the arm I was holding the bag with then guided me down the corridor.

Whats the matter? she hissed.

The bus goes at ten, I says and walked out, then I turned and kneeled down to the bag. I shoved aside clothes till I pulled out the envelope and gave Lanna the rest of my cash.

Whats this? she goes.

Take it, I'm splitting.

Youre what? says Lanna.

I'm going elsewhere; heres this and have a good time but take care, theres about a hundred there.

Where are you going; why are you always having to be so dramatic about everything Morvern?

I just looked at her.

I mean are you still beeling about Him or what is it this time? I mean I thought you were into all this. Used to be you were the life of the party, none of us could keep up with you. Why dont you just get tore into having a good time rather than this daft brooding? If you are going cant I come; I mean is it me you hate?

I dont hate anyone Lanna.

You just dont know what youre thinking Morvern, she says.

I nodded.

I walked down the stairs smiling straight away. I crossed the road in front of the hotel and walked up the pavement to the bank. It was very cool inside and the folk behind the counter had music going on a radio.

I signed every one of the traveller's cheques then folded the big dollop of purplish notes into my shoulder bag.

Round by the fountain I chose the taxi with a lady driver.

Up the coast, away from here, I says.

The lady taxi driver bunched up her forehead and goes, Eh?

I pointed my hand and goes, North.

All morning we drove up the veering road through ports with churches. Painted fishing boats were dragged up stony beaches and we went through orchards of orange and lemon trees with deep dark greeny leaves.

We stopped for lunch in a hotel by the sea. Cloth napkins and silver on the table. The taxi driver had a small glass of wine and fish then coffee. I says, Champagne please, your best make. I had an omelette made and the chef in a hat carried it to our table by the windows. The taxi driver and me couldnt speak, though she did to the waiter.

When we left I put on my sunglasses. I paid in cash and

as a reminder I carried the smooth rounded black empty champagne bottle with me.

In the afternoon we come down a twisty road among pine trees. Villas were clustered all over the hills around a resort so much smaller than where I'd been. When I paid the taxi driver she kissed me each cheek and goes, Bye bye, in my words.

I booked into the Mirabel Hotel near the harbour. I had a room with shutters painted paleish blue and chipped. Scales of silver vibrated on the ceiling reflected offof the sea below. You heard the chink of cutlery and low words of folk having lunch on the terrace underneath. I put the champagne bottle on the tallboy.

I got out of the dress and in the swimsuit then put the dress on top, got my towel and walked down onto the beach.

Across the sand I let the dress fall, folded it then stepped right into the water. Shallow in it was luke-warm. I stood and scrunched up my toes gripping sand in them. I walked out deeper till it touched my belly button. The swell was really low but the surface lifted up a little on my tummy and I was holding my arms high out of the water. When it splashed under my bosoms I dived forward, blew out and kicked up to the surface. I twisted onto my back then tugged wet hair out of my face; I floated with the sun just going on forehead and cheeks. When I turned my head aside, the water was so clear you saw all dune-shapes on the sandy bottom: a seabed of sand under water that was the colour blue, like in brochures.

I tread water and looked in. Where you would expect a jumble of hills and a circular folly above a port: none. Where you would expect piers with a seawall between and an esplanade of hotels beyond: none. Where you would expect stone houses hunched round a horseshoe of bay with The Complex tucked away round a back: none. The resort I was looking at was really another place.

I looked up to the north: a long height of land with the harbour under its slope and windmills along the plateau edge. Veering road zig-zigged between summerhouses built up in steps above the harbour. The plateau stretched into the sea putting its big blunt end right out with green currents coming from the cliff bottoms below the lighthouse at the top.

The harbour was to my side, a long causeway made of big concrete blocks guys were fishing off. You could see the fishing boats on the protected side.

To the south of the Mirabel was a stretch of rock and past it a curve of beach that turned into more high cliffs way along. Behind the curve of beach were the roofs of bars and restaurants then behind their telly aerials the hazy greeny-blackishness of low hills with painted-white villas scattered like bones all over them.

I looked at the apartment buildings. You saw the skeleton of one apartment building that wasnt finished with its four floors and stairs.

I started swimming in then stood when my feet could touch the bottom. When I was back in the hotel room I washed my face in the sink then used a peel-off-mask-with-cucumber. I lay back on the bed to let my face dry.

I was just looking at the ceiling and how the light was changed. It wasnt scales of silver vibrating on it: it was glow from a sunset. When the mask was dry all over I got in front the mirror and peeled the thin film back away from my forehead and down till I'd a skin of my nose and cheeks shape, inside out. I threw the mask of my face shape into the toilet and jerked the flush.

When I walked out in the décolleté top the night air was very clear. There was the white colouredness from the lighthouse turning round and round but as I walked along the front in the warm air you saw another light jabbering over the orchards behind the apartments. It was a strobe light pulsing again and again so's I started the walking towards it.

You could hear the music echoing up the dry riverbed before you got there. All the cars seemed a same colour cause of night and the strobe light that sent out its message from right up on top of the old windmill that the club was built round. Outside, a neon sign gave a list of the ambient DJs on till six in the morning: DJ Sacaea and The Spook Factory Night. Beside the windmill were these big iron doors the security kept pulling aside. I looked across to the cliffs where a creamy paleish moon was lifting up then I walked into the club.

In morning I lay nude on top the sheets just watching the

shimmers reflecting offof the ceiling. You could hear the cutlery below the shutters and also the waves lushing up on the sand. I stretched out an arm and turned the waterproof watch towards me. I swung my legs round and let them dangle over the bedside. I did a deep breath.

In the evening after all the salad and Fanta on the terrace I walked up the long road that separated the resort from the village. The lampposts had flags and bunting hanging between them.

Deep in the village the streets were so narrow you could have reached out from one window and held hands with the person in the house across. The sounds carried round corners from a good few streets down so it was a mystery where whispered voices came from.

I had walked through the village following the procession of people on the inland road across the dry places towards the villages of Poor Jesus and St Michael In Excelsis. The procession and drummers moved up a steep little hill to the bright white chapel at the top. I climbed up the path among the sharp rocks and olive trees. Though the sun was going down and it was cooler, I was breathing fast. No one talked and you could see more people making their way up the road from the harbour.

It was dark and you smelt smoke from the burning torches the men carried. Little girls in black lace were holding hands with girls in white lace behind the men with the torches.

The strongest-looking fishermen disappeared through the doors of the chapel. The words All Hills Are Calvary were over the top of the wooden doors with other words for this in all different languages.

Slowly, on a throne and litter that rested on the shoulders of the fishermen, the pale model of the virgin saint girl seemed to float out the chapel in her heavy lace dress with tinkling bells. She was as tall as me. I stared at her face as she passed.

The procession began to move back down the rocky path following her. It was so dark up away from the streets the torch bearers lit the way through the scrub with the drummers following.

We moved through the narrow village streets where teenage girls reached out from balconies trying to touch the model girl. When we passed the home for the blind I saw all the old ladies dressed in black, feeling their way round the walls in the torch light. You saw the way the blind old women were holding their heads casting shadow down the wall: they were listening for her bells tinkling on the lace dress.

The procession reached the harbour and the girl was carried up to a newfangled-looking contraption of a building. It was the fisherpeople's church made from folded concrete on the outside.

Inside, the girl was carried to the top end. When you looked up to the ceiling there was a strip of blueish glass round the top of the walls and the moonlight was lighting up the glass so's the colour showed on faces. The roof wasnt flat: it was made of varnished wooden planks that came to a point way above heads: it was in the shape of a boat's keel. The whole roof was the wooden hull of a fishing boat a hundred feet above. With the light filtering in you were already drowned and on the bottom of the deep sea with the living people above.

The church bells started ringing when the procession came out. More people held up torches. Fireworks started bursting above the cliffs and in front of the moon. Rockets were getting shot from a circle of anchored fishing boats in the harbour basin.

The girl's face was getting lit by the different coloured rockets exploding above. She was lifted onto a huge raft decorated in tinsel with candles burning under glass covers. The raft had an engine fitted and it was radio controlled. The men guided the raft out the harbour and it moved smoothly across the water with her sitting up erect.

When she was moving further out to sea the men pushed a button. Suddenly the raft began to smoke and then flames appeared round the base.

It burned very quick. The flames came flickering out of the darkness smearing a long line of light across the water towards everybody. A spiral of flame was lifting up from her hair then in a cloud of steam the raft capsized and sank.

I began walking towards the strobe of the nightclub then I turned back to the hotel.

During the night you heard the odd firework still go off and the waves on the sand.

At dawn when I swam out I found young girls in masks already there swimming in circles trying to see her burned face looking up at us from the seabed below.

I LOOKED OUT the hotel window and cement mixers were hanging from cranes high above the darkened building sites so's they wouldnt get thieved. Low down, planes moved across the skyline.

I was still unpacked sat on the edge of the bed when that editor, Tom Bonnington from the book company, knocked on the door. There was a woman with him. He goes, Hey, hi it's great to finally meet you.

Hiya, I went.

Hows the room, okay? he says.

Aye. Amazing thanks, I goes.

Well this is Susan from the design side of things, she wants a word with you about covers.

Covers, I went looking over at the bed.

The cover to the novel.

Oh aye.

The Susan smiled and before she'd even says hello goes, I think you've written an amazing first novel. It's really, really heavy. I've some ideas for the cover we could throw around later.

Have a good time on holiday then? says Tom.

I turned to look at him then nod-nodded.

Susan goes, I try to get over every few years to see how it's changing, but it's finding the time isnt it?

I went, Aye.

Have you been to the Alhambra in Granada? goes Susan.

What kind of music is it there? I says.

Theres no music, Susan went.

Ah, I goes.

It's a moorish palace, Tom says.

I says, I was just on the rave scene.

There was a bit of silentness then Tom punched his palm and goes, Well Morvern, I thought this evening we could go out, even hit a club maybe?

Got a car? I says.

No, we thought we might be drinking, goes Susan.

Oh. Aye, I went then I sniffed.

Or would you sooner we stayed in and had a chat about the book? says Tom.

No, no, just I'm sort of a bit short, I goes.

Pardon?

I'm a bit broke, y'know?

Oh you mean money?

Aye, sort of a bit low on the money side of things.

Tom laughed from across that hotel room and I looked at him as he says, Well I'm sure the company can stretch to a pizza and some drinks.

I was really wondering could I tap yous fifteen or twenty till I get home then I'll square up? I goes.

Well how about your rail fare? went Tom.

Thats free anyway cause my fosterdad works on the railway.

Pardon?

My fosterdad works on the railway so's his family gets the free travel; he's a driver.

Ah, I see, you get privileged travel?

Privileged? Well it's free, I goes.

Well of course I can lend you twenty, says Tom.

Oh, right then, great, thats really kind, I went.

You cant get much from working in a supermarket, goes Susan.

Well thats right, says Tom counting out two tens from a wallet with a stack in as well as the different colours of credit cards.

Thanks very much Tom.

Tom says, I know the advance on the book wasnt much but that can always change. Have you been working on any new material?

Sorry?

Have you been working on material?

Material?

You'll get that final payment for your book when it's out at the end of the summer then the royalties will come in at the end of the tax year.

Royalties? I goes.

Yes. There are subsidiary rights too; in America it's seventy-five per cent if anything ever came to anything, says Tom.

Susan says, You know what they say dont you?

I turned and looked at her.

She says, Time tells if you are great but Royalties if you are popular.

Tom and Susan both laughed. I nodded. They talked so constant you found their blethers made less sense than locals back in the resort but you found you could get by with a Uh huh, a Mmm, giving the odd nod or coming out with a chuckle and that.

We took the lift down to the cocktail bar where I bought me and Susan Southern Comfort with lemonade. Tom had this beer and the bottle was wrapped in tissue paper. There were saucers with cocktail cherries on sticks and saucers of chocolate buttons just sitting on the bar. I was hungry so I started putting one cherry after another into my mouth till there was just a pile of cocktail sticks left. When I looked over I saw them watching me like hawks. I smiled and waved then kept chewing up the big mouthful of so delicious cherries in my mouth. I carried over their drinks then when I went back to get my own I took one of the saucers of chocolate buttons with me.

Yous should see the big fish tank in the foyer and, would you believe it, there's an actual nail salon here too, I says. There was a bit silentness so I chewed up one button till it was a melted ball then I pushed out the mush on the tip of my tongue and smeared the paste between two solid buttons making a wee chocolate button sandwich. Those two were watching me so I did a big breath then says, See, I do the books myself cause of the lifestyle that goes with it, y'know? The writers sit there smoking and go round looking for the inspiration. It's a lifestyle thats got a lot to offer me, much better than working in a supermarket; waking up on cold mornings knowing it's thirty-nine years to go till pension. When youre writing you can just knock off, take a look out the window, make a cup of coffee or have a shower.

They'd both leaned forward and were nodding at me. I offered round the cigarettes but they didnt smoke. I used the goldish lighter on a Silk Cut.

We had another round of drinks then we walked out the hotel and down a street. Tom was trying to hail a taxi. A double-decker came along so I got on cause I'd never been on one before. They had to climb on too but they were both explaining how they never took the bus and they showed me these Taxi Card things that meant they could just use taxis any time without even having money. They had no change for the bus, just tenners, so I had to pay for three tickets.

As we got off the double-decker outside the nightclub two women who looked like cleaners got out the doors in front of Tom and Susan. You saw both women just nod heads to the driver but not up the aisle cause they understood the driver wouldnt be looking there. The women nodded up to the big rounded mirror the driver would be watching the door in. Susan says, Thank you driver, then stepped off carefully. I nodded in the mirror.

Tom got us in and the music was so brilliantly loud it

put paid to any ceilidhing. The DJ was playing Dreamfish mixed in with other sounds. I was up dancing the whole length and breadth of the dancefloor before Susan got the first round in.

Elbows bent towards chest and fingers bunched, I stepped to the side during drum breaks. I turned my ankles then moved fast through lasers. A good instance of that would have been during Earthworm by Spiral Tribe Sound System. Stopped, I hunched over a Silk Cut using the goldish lighter, swaying from side to side taking the odd step forward till all was smoked. A boy had stepped up to me and says something but I just turned my back. I dropped the cigarette end and bent elbows towards chest again.

When I sat at the table I was covered in sweat. It was just running down my arms from under the waistcoat. Susan had got a bottle of champagne up on the table so I leaned across and gave her a big hug. Tom draped these five luminous whistles round my neck: you got one each time you bought a round of drinks but they got five for a bottle of champagne. The music was so loud all we did was smile at each other, raise our plastic cups and watch the dancers on the floor.

Tom passed something to Susan and she nodded to the toilets.

We had to wait for a cubicle and when the door opened two girls came out laughing. I locked the door then we sniffed this little bit white powder Susan had. I lifted up my leg to show her the glittering knee. I used the goldish lighter to make it sparkle as Susan just stared at it without talking.

When the champagne was drunk we moved on to another club. There was no house music just all these twelve inches and remixes. The guy behind the bar told us the club owner could only get the black marble for the bar from a stonemason who made graves and if you felt under the rim where I was standing you could feel an abandoned inscription. I ran my fingers under and it was right enough; we were leaned against all these gravestones.

Tom got us a taxi to this late place that served food. In the back I was feeling right queer. Hotness would gather in my face but then it seemed to move out of my face if I concentrated on it, leaving me dizzy. Like when something went across me, my lips had a numb feeling and I kept turning my suntanned face to see its reflection in the little mirror. When I stared at my face it wasnt like you were where your reflection showed you. Then the flush came back. I shook my left arm and did a big breath.

We clambered out the taxi. There was a war memorial right next to us. I was reading out loud the words engraved on it: Yser, Loos, Arras, Lille, Struma, Vimi, Hoole, Mons, Hill 60.

Really good nicknames you give your people down here, I says.

Beg pardon? goes Tom.

The nicknames of these dead soldiers were great, I says.

Those are not nicknames, those are the names of the battles, went Tom.

Oh, I goes.

The place was called Sunrise and we sat at a table near the door. There was a strange rule that for every pound you spent on drink you had to spend two pound on food. About twenty uneaten, cold plates of chips were sitting on our table, across the floor and round about us on spare seats. We were all mortal as newts. Tom was using his credit cards to buy more drink and plates of chips that I was handing to people as they came in the door.

Tom or Susan would ask a question looking at you, you would shrug your shoulders with a bottle of beer in the mouth and they would answer the question themselves then argue about it. They didnt tell stories they just discussed.

When Susan asked Tom to stop yapping so she could hear me talking it was: All I know is over there in that resort, with a couple of thousand pounds, happiness was as easy as your first breath in the morning, that Susan heard me say.

In actual fact the dawn was begun on the skyline when we left Sunrise and started the walking up a street. We mustve been further from the airport cause the planes were higher up. Tom's tie was skew-iff and his jacket was over Susan's shoulders.

We came to a church. I put my fingers up to my lips to tell them: shush.

Inside was dark with candles up the far end where an actual early-morning mass was going on.

Tom and Susan suddenly started snogging, Tom's jacket slid off Susan's shoulders and lay on the flagstones. Her bum was pushed up against the thing with the holy water in. An old woman came in and scowled almightily at the two of them as she squeezed round to dap her fingers wet and cross herself. When she says words to the two snoggers it was in foreign language.

I wet my fingers and crossed myself then looked down the aisle to watch the old woman and see what knee you genuflect on. A handsome black priest was about to give the Eucharist. Candlelight reflected on his skin.

Tom and Susan followed me up the aisle. I genuflected then slid along a bench. They copy-catted and sat in beside me. When folk all started going up I rose first with Susan behind me. I took her hand.

Two young foreign girls with haversacks on were in front of us. I watched their stiff-looking little tongues take the wafers.

I kneeled and when the priest touched my head with long thin fingers I swayed as if I was going to faint. I squeezed my eyes tight for a split second then I took the wafer with its taste in my mouth. Tom and Susan copied, then followed me back where I was kneeling on the row of cushions behind the benches. I screwed my eyes shut tight and had a little prayer.

Outside it was daylightish.

Oh, that was so really, really *heavy*, Susan kept repeating. Her arm was linked with Tom's. We crossed the road and I just drifted into an underground station. I jerked aside the curtain and all three of us squeezed into a photo-booth laughing. Tom began passing all these pound coins to me so I hunkered down in the short skirt trying to get them in the slot. Flashes started going off so we were all in hysterics, twisting and crouching to get in the shot with our cheeks all squeezed together. We were doing this for a good while then Tom's coins fell on the floor. I scraped them together with my trainer then pushed all the pound coins in the slot. More flashes started going off.

Susan reached round to touch my glittering knee and I held my head back as she stroked it so my hair hung in her face while she sat on Tom's knee on the stool. Another hand came round and moved up the inside of the leg. I could taste the wafer in my mouth. A flash crackled and both my palms shot up and pressed against the plastic light cover on the roof. My heart was going twenty to the dozen and Susan says in a hushed way, Oh my god, this is so heavy.

I was starting to speak about the raves I'd been going to at Spook Factory when I saw Susan's face was all pale. It was just then the jet of boak came out her mouth and nose across Tom's shoes. Another flash bloomed. I tried to lift Susan up but only so's she was in a position where the camera would take her all sicking up. The next splut of sick was a huge amount and hit the glass plate where the camera was.

Tom was soothing her and saying stuff, but wetness

was pouring down Susan's front onto the thighs of his trousers. I stepped outside the booth: a whole series of photos were piled up on the concrete. I picked them up, took out the rampant ones then chucked the others back down. I'd an early train to get and my bag was still at that hotel.

The train climbed back west then east through the evening and away from The Central Belt. As far as the crossing loop it was a Central Belt train driver. The train back to the port would cross at the loop with the 17.40 on its way down, then a port driver would take the train back along above the lochs, through to the junction and up the glens and across to the far end of the pass, over the back hills and round into the port.

The coach I was in behind the engine jerked to a halt. Everything was very quiet except for a little creaking under the carriage and a tiny burn gurgle-gurgling by the trackside.

You heard a lonely horn blow and a diesel growling. For a split second Coll was beside; sitting up in the engine cab when the train from the port slowed and stopped next me.

I picked up my bag then crossed to the coach door and pulled the window down. It was starting to drizzle. Coll was coming up the platform with Woofit his dog running in front then circling.

Coll!

Morvern. Morvern youre the talk of the town; where on earth have you disappeared to. Are you coming up then?

I opened the door and got down.

Have you phoned; have you heard about Red Hanna?

What, him retiring?

Oh Morvern have you no been in touch at all, come here, come here, the big white chiefs have got him. Suspended his lump sum and pension on a discipline.

I looked at Coll. A feeling was going across me. We were stood by the engine near the cab door. Coll tugged the silver-coloured handle down and jerked the door in. Woofit hopped up. Coll put a hand on each rail and eased himself up into the engine. I stepped on quickly and snapped the door behind me. Coll swung his big leather bag onto the diesely floor beside the driver's seat. I sat on the other swivel chair.

Coll says, The devils sent him out a letter on yon Friday saying that he'd taken two lager shandies that last afternoon he was backshift 'fore going out on his final train.

Two lager shandies, I goes.

Worse than pathetic, eh, went Coll spreading out the centre pages of his newspaper on the floor that Woofit curled up on.

Surely management know that worse than that goes on at Hogmanay, I says.

I know pet, I've been carried to the engine myself but they love to get an old commy and union activist. Set

Red Hanna up nice they did. It's total rubbish, the management turn a blind eye when it suits them, goes Coll taking out the Tupperware box and unwrapping the can of dogfood then scraping some out onto a saucer that Woofit gobbled down. Then Coll did a rolly with his silver box. I used the goldish lighter on a Silk Cut then leaned over to give Coll a light.

Ta, how long have you been AWOL now? went Coll.

Week and six days the morrow. Heard anything about my job?

Coll raised his eyebrows and says, It's no looking too rosy Morvern, The Creeping Jesus phoned Red Hanna after two days.

Tsch, I went.

Where the hell've you been? says Coll.

I shrugged then went, Dancing and lying on the beach till my money ran out then a night in London.

Aye well, while youre young, laughed Coll. He crossed to the door and tugged it open behind my seat. He leaned out the door waiting for the guard's signal, Right thats us, he says.

Coll crossed back to the driver's place after slamming the door. He sat down in the driver's seat and you saw his arm move underneath: the horn thumped below our feet. He tapped a handle back that let out a hiss of air then thunked the other forward. He moved the big handle back a little and the engine whined up behind us. The din in the cab from the engine room behind would be too much for any talking till Coll shut off for the long run down to the isthmus. Any talking would be regulated all the way to the port by when the engine would be screaming away, cause of gradients, so loud it's almost frightening, or ticking over down hills and carrying us along glens with the thud thud thud of wheels underneath.

I was going to say something but there was no point. We were shaking round that long straight before the pass. Woofit was up and about and I'd poured him a bit water. Coll moved the handle then the engine whirled up. The cylinders above both windscreens hissed as they moved the wipers. I looked up to the top of the stairs and the hotel with the pointing-up tower, the graveyard path beyond and the tips of the pines where the Tree Church would be, the petals from the bower fallen to the grass in that rain. Further along past the Falls platform, at the edge of the ridge the waterfalls were tipping over but it looked like there was a load of bonfires on the ridge. The wind was blowing so fierce the waterfalls were being blown backwards over the ridge-edge in clouds.

We moved east to the Back Settlement then in west till we came in behind The Complex and down into the port through the long cutting by the signal box. With both hands I pulled down the cab window; the port looked same as ever round the bay. The cab swayed a little and a hiss came from the brake handle as Coll nudged it over. As we ran along the platform edge I swung the seat round and bent down to pick up the bag. Woofit was up, circling and wagging his tail. The engine stopped moving and there was a dying honk of air as Coll snapped down the worn reddish-painted handle on the cab wall behind him. I opened the cab door and Woofit was out the train engine and sniffing around the passengers who were crowded up against the gate with Zipper checking tickets. I jumped down onto the platform.

Coll stood up in the cab doorway shouting Woofit away from the passengers. Coll sniffed and says, Mmm the only time these machines smell good is after youve been in them Morvern Callar.

I laughed and goes, I'd best be shooting, thanks for the hurl.

Aye no bother, no bother, you'd best away and find that man.

He'll be on the sesh.

No surprised. You take care you crazy thing.

You too, bye Woofit, I goes, kneeling and giving the dog a good clapping round the ears.

I crossed the square then looked up. There was still time to make it to the superstore.

Once across the carpark I moved through the sliding door and past the signing book. You saw The Seacow who was alone on tills turn and stare. I took the door up to the ladies' staffroom and Creeping Jesus's office. The staffroom was empty so I used the key on my locker then pushed aside the nylon uniform and the tights in a ball. I took out the schoolish shoes then rummaged through the shelf. I took a few things; make-up, a bottle paracetamol and vitamins, then put them in my bag.

I walked through, knocked on Creeping Jesus's door then stepped in.

Well, well, look whos arrived, our own suntanned supermodel, Creeping Jesus says.

There was a long bit of silentness.

Going to tell me why youre two weeks late for work then? Creeping Jesus says.

Thirteen days, I goes.

It's not just me suffers you know Morvern, the whole section suffers, working a man short.

I'm not a man.

Dont get smart.

Well I'm not, I went then coughed.

Where've you been?

Thats none of your business just tell me where I stand, have I got a job? Cause if I dont then why should I be stood in your office like this?

What do you think Morvern?

Fine, I goes.

It was the orangey plastic chair that always sat by the door I threw across his office at him. A back leg hit the front of the desk so the chair made a wobbling noise and shot off into the corner of the room. Creeping Jesus had got crouched down behind the desk, shouting about police.

Away crawl under the stone you came from, Creeping

Jesus, I says. I wrenched the door open so bad-temperedly it crashed into the filing cabinets.

I walked out into the carpark, used the goldish lighter on a Silk Cut under one of the lights then crossed The Black Lynn that flows under the port.

In the night, rain was spotting down from the light's haloes. I walked into Haddows, asked for a half bottle voddy and counted out more of the money yon Tom and Susan subbed me.

I walked quick up past Video Rental, St John's then the Phoenix. Cars were circling the port roads with elbows out windows. I dug my house keys from the bag.

On the mat were seven catalogues from model shops in the south and the letter with a queer postmark addressed to me. I picked them all up and dropped them on His desk. I put De Devil Dead by Lee Perry on the CD then I towelled my hair and twisted it up into a French roll. I put on the heater and immerser.

I'd forgot to get something for diluting the voddy and of course the fridge was bare so I opened this bottle of sweet wine and used that to dilute it. There was a can tinned potatoes so I opened it, drained the can then popped the potatoes in my mouth one after the other. While chewing I was just staring at the black window.

When that immerser had heated I gulped some more of the bogging-tasting drink then stripped in front the fire, standing on one leg of the wet jeans to tug the other foot out.

After shaving my legs and having a good bath I used

every clean towel on me and put SDI on the CD. In-the-scud with that religious music going I got down on the polished floorboards and tried hard with a wee prayer. I suddenly jumped up and paraded about all agitated. I took out De Devil Dead and put in From The Secret Laboratory by Lee Perry. I flicked forward to tracks 6 and 7. This time the praying went an awful lot better and when I'd finished I was shivering with perished coldness.

I got dressed then put on the steerhide jacket from the wardrobe. I drank some more voddy then got the brolly and headed outside.

The wind tugged at the brolly and drops vibrated offof the edge as I hunched under.

I walked towards the phonebox, took the brolly down and got in. There was no answer at The Complex. I phoned V the D's out the Back Settlement.

Hello 206, she goes.

It's Morvern.

Morvern where are you? Your father's worried sick about you as if he doesnt have enough of his own problems.

I'm home.

We thought you'd been kidnapped or something.

Where is he then?

He's there in the port tonight. I've told him not to worry, I mean we'll get by, might have to put off the extension. Have you been to work?

Aye. Sacked.

Oh Morvern, she sighed and laughed, What are we going to do with the Callars? Surely you'll get a bit hotel work before the end of season?

The pips started and I looked up at the ceiling.

Morvern . . .?

I put the phone down softly and listened to the rain on the roof of the box. I pushed out the door.

I used the shortcut up to the circular folly trying not to go skiteing in the runny mud. From the top of Jacob's Ladder I looked down on the port and the fishing boats tied up at the pier. I tried to look behind The Complex towards the mountains where the pass goes west to the village beyond the power station but there were only the moving clouds above orangey street light.

Going down Jacob's Ladder I tried to miss the puddles. Water was splattering over from the cliff above. No couples kissed on the benches of each platform. I looked down on the dark street under the cliff and the dull lights of Red Hanna's local: The Politician Hotel.

I pushed open the door and shook water off the steerhide jacket's arms. All heads turned and followed me as I walked to the fridge where not only was Povie the butcher's extra meat kept but the Politician had placed the pool table cause it wouldnt fit anywhere else. I stuck my head in: five men were round the table, two were playing. A big hunk of meat was hung from one of the hooks and a man was holding it aside so the player could take a good shot. The other men were puffing into their hands.

Look it's one of the strippers, says a guy in a boilersuit.

Shh, thats yon engine driver's girl, another went as I turned round, stepped up to the bar and goes, Has Red Hanna been in the night?

A week past Friday, goes a voice behind me. I turned round.

An old greyhead was sat with tears coming from his eyes that he kept dabbing with a hanky. He was far from greeting though and it was a double he had in front him.

I'm Tod the Post, youre Morvern, Red Hanna's girl, you work in the superstore, eh?

Not any more I dont. Have you seen him then?

Not since he was in yon time, no like him to neglect us for so long.

Any inkling where he'll be?

Havent the foggiest. You'd be best parking yourself here and making an old fool happy; whats your pleasure?

Nah, I couldnt get you back.

Ah, sit yourself down. Red Hanna would skin me if he hears youve been in and no treated well. It's The Weekday Club the night, a' bhailaich, get the girl with the smashing suntan a drink.

A Southern Comfort and lemonade please, I goes.

A what? says the barman.

Southern Comfort?

We dont have that here.

I looked at the bottles and says, A Sweetheart Stout please.

I sat beside Tod the Post. The guys through the fridge door were betting loudly on a pool game.

A bunch of folk came in, all a bit younger, soaked to the skin and carrying packages. Tod the Post nudged and goes, Look, The Weekday Club.

The folk settled at a bench, started dividing up a loaf with a penknife and cutting a big block of processed cheese.

Tod the Post says, Feeding of the five thousand, still got our soup kitchens in this neck of the woods; theyre on the dole so we all chip in fifty pence and come dance night we have ourselves a little buffet.

One of the older Weekday Club shouted, That your granddaughter, Post?

No, no this is Red Hanna's daughter.

Oh, up the revolution then, we'll support yous but it's up to you young ones to bring it about.

Aye, we'll be behind you, Tod the Post says.

I nodded.

Are you looking for your Father dear?

Aye, I goes.

Have you no heard the scandal? Know where you'll find him the night, half the holy willies are up the street there. They've got strippers up at The Mantrap the night, you'll find all the railway there, eh? laughs this older woman.

One of the guys from the fridge came through and says, Will I start taking the light shades down?

Aye, goes the barman.

The guy from the fridge stood up on the long seat row and started unscrewing the glass shades on the lights above the seats. Some other locals started getting up to help him.

Whats that for? I says.

So we can get up on the seats and dance when the ceilidh really starts going, says Tod the Post.

Aye? I went, laughing.

The other guys round the pool table in the fridge had stopped playing and put the balls on the floor in the triangle. The guy in the boilersuit took a ferret out, let it slither from hand to hand then he popped the ferret down the middle pocket of the pool table. You saw the ferret dash past the glass. The men were betting as to what pocket the ferret would emerge from.

Here, I goes leaning across to the old treasurer with a fifty p.

She handed me a thick bit bread and cheese then says, Thats you paid up for next week too.

Right, I nodded taking a bite into the piece. I finished the Sweetheart Stout. I was starting to warm up among all the blethering.

I'm off then, I says getting up.

Well then, hope you find him, went Tod the Post.

Same time next week, goes The Weekday Club woman.

Right-oh, I says.

See you next week unless theres a revolution before then, went the woman, laughing.

Aye, unless, I goes.

I put the brolly up outside The Politician then walked

round the corner and down to the seawall. Wind was whistling and the sea sometimes blasting against the wall so the circling traffic swung away at the worst bit where some seaweed and a fishbox were lying on the road. Spray was hitting against the bakery windows and a couple ministers in shiny sou'westers and shepherds' coats were outside The Mantrap.

Abandon hope all you who enter, shouted one of the ministers.

I always do, I snapped back at him.

It was stifling and chock-a-block inside. Everyone was there, usual men, usual boys with their usual faces and usual bums.

Hey, Skinny-ma-linky-long-legs with the suntan, Lanna shouted.

I turned and she was squeezing between folk with a tray of drinks.

Have you been to the work? she gasped.

Aye, I totally blew it.

Where the hell've you been; raving?

Aye.

Whats it like up the coast?

Queer, weirder; I've had some mental times.

How did you get back? Lanna says.

I was at this resort with an airport near, theres scheduled flights to the capital and that; it's easy if youve the money.

Any left?

No ways; remember our promise?

Aye, Lanna laughed.

Never come back from holiday with a penny in the purse eh? I didnt either. I spent everything; had to borrow money off these London folk.

Boys?

Nut, just idiots.

Lanna says, I've bad news.

Aye, I know, I come up in the front of the train with Coll.

Eh? Lanna went.

Red Hanna's discipline.

Nah, nah I'm no meaning that, Granny Couris Jean died the day after we left for the resort.

I gave Lanna a look. After a good bit I says, I mean, what happened?

Just took to her bed one morning and my Mum sat with her through the night till she went. She was over ninety.

Thats just awful, I goes.

You havent really been about when we all needed you Morvy, I mean you could have phoned.

I nodded and says, I cant explain; over there it's weird, it's queer, then I shook my head.

I looked up and says, Have you seen Dad?

He's here, went Lanna.

Whereabouts?

Here, goes Lanna nodding to the drinks tray.

Oh, I went.

I mean you just werent here when he needed you, Lanna goes.

I followed her over and Red Hanna was at one of the wee round tables; soon as he saw me he stood up laughing and kissed me on the side of my face.

Some tan, says Red Hanna.

Aye, I goes.

Heard all the news?

I came up with Coll. I reckon I've lost my job; in fact I know I've lost it. I'll go sign on the morrow.

Look, you and Lanna could share the flat, I'd help yous out when I could, this thing, it's just a temporary thing, the union'll fight it to the death. Red Hanna smiled at Lanna.

Lanna offered round a pack of Regals so I took and used the goldish lighter round the table.

There was a long bit of silentness as I blew out smoke.

Well here we are, says Lanna.

Aye, went Red Hanna. He was on pints and nips but he tipped a slosh of his pint into an empty glass and Lanna scraped the glass across the table towards me. I nodded. A sort of feeling was starting to go across me.

Tell Morvy about the stripper, says Lanna.

Red Hanna says, It was crazy, just men were in, about a hundred, Hiphearan and The Panatine and Mockit with all their mad fisher mates; men had come over from the island and taken their sons. On she come and I'm not joking, The Slab had to stop it.

How come? I goes.

They were going to rape her for sure, the lassie was terrified, just you and Lanna's age. So The Slab comes on the stage and tells the guys down the front to screw the head or no more girl. Course then there was near a riot. All the fishermen were bawling, Is she a nun or something, is she a nun? The Slab tells them to keep their hands to themselves. Well the fishermen are booing and hissing then suddenly that Panatine is up, turning his back to the stage and shaking his head then the nutter starts taking *his* clothes off and he just sits back at his table beside the stage. Course his mates are all in hysterics at The Panatine and you know what that lot are like, all on some kind of drugs; so then *they* all start coming off with the clothes as well, about thirty of them naked down by the stage. When the girl comes on doing her thing to the music the boys dont even so much as look at her, the men just sit there completely in-the-scud, playing cards and chatting like she was invisible. The Panatine even goes up and buys a tray of drinks. Youve never seen anything so mad, the lassie couldnt of known what kind of nut house she was in.

What a shame for her, I says.

Ah, no place like the port, goes Red Hanna.

I turned to Lanna and I says, Did Couris Jean say anything before she died?

Say anything? Lanna went.

Aye.

Lanna goes, Queerly enough Mum was saying she kept

talking before she went to sleep, the same words again and again.

What words, does your Mum remember? I says.

Lanna gave me a look and went, Nah, cause Couris Jean's last words were in Gaelic and my Mum doesnt know any Gaelic.

A bigger sort of feeling went across me for some reason. Red Hanna moved up to get a round of drinks. When he came back he'd got two Southern Comforts and lemonade but you could tell Lanna's was a double.

I'm just going to the toilet, I says.

I locked the cubicle and sat on the toilet with the face in the hands letting out the huffs. When I walked back through you saw them lean apart.

I sat and looked at the floor between my feet. I could see Lanna was sat the same way. I swallowed, sniffed, a shiver went across me and I says, Sub us a fiver then and I'll get a round in.

Mortal and getting drenched, the three of us made our way up past Video Rental, St John's, the Bayview and the Phoenix. Lanna was holding on Red Hanna's arm. She broke off and stopped to let me catch up. She flung an arm over my shoulder then just says, Morvy can we use your room cause V the D's always phoning The Complex; we can't get any peace?

Aye, do as yous like, I says.

Are you okay?

Yup.

Wait till I move in and that, we'll have a great time, she says.

They both waited while I unlocked the door and led the way in. I started boiling the kettle. Before the switch clicked off Lanna and my fosterdad were snogging on the couch.

Near their feet I cooried down in front the CD and put on Unlimited Edition by The Can. When I keeked over my shoulder you could see right the way up Lanna's leg. You heard the couch cushions doing that rustling then Gomorrha (Dec 73) started.

Red Hanna got up and moved through to the toilet; you heard the splattering. Lanna was sat looking at me then she says, Want a lend of a tenner?

Aye okay then, I says.

Lanna took it out and put it on the table.

Red Hanna came back through. I looked him right in the face and he says, You dont even like Vanessa.

I stood up, walked through to the toilet and locked the door.

When I came out you heard TV Spot (April 1971) and them laugh through in my bedroom. I sat on the couch, saw Lanna had left her Regals so I lit one. I stood and picked up the catalogues and that letter with the queer postmark from offof His desk. I plonked the catalogues in the bonzo.

I just tore open the envelope and read down the typed

lines of words. I looked straight up across the room to the light gap of the bedroom door.

I read the lines of words again.

I brought the letter down to beside my thigh and its paper fluttered. The Empress And The Ukraine King (Jan 1969) was starting.

I lifted the letter again to read it the once more.

In two steps I was at the boiler cupboard. I pulled it open and tugged down some folded towels onto the floor. With both arms held up I lifted out the old brown suitcase then swung round and set it down over by the record player. I opened the top of the case then started flicking through the collection. You could tell the difference between a CD's click: heavier and quick, or a cassette: softer with a hollowness. Records folded with a puff. Every so often I layered a record from His or my collection into the case. Sometimes I tossed in a cassette or CD. I pulled out my toilet bag from the holiday bag.

I crossed to the desk, reached under then switched on the plug. On His computer I typed up on screen:

AWAY RAVING. DONT BE WORRYING ABOUT ME.
SELL EVERYTHING HERE.
MORVERN

Connection (March 1969) was playing on the machine. I put it off, took out the CD and shut it in the cover then threw it into the case. I clipped the case shut and tried to lift it. It wasnt too bad but you heard all the cassettes clatter down the bottom.

I took out the letter from His solicitors and skipped all the bit about transferring directly into my account and all the stuff about taxation. There was a bit about His solicitors wanting me to pass on His latest Contact Address. There was the bit about them being able to Advise me if I had Investment in mind as the Office had Many Years' Experience and were Able To Advise me. I read the amount the Tax Office had finally let them transfer into my branch account.

I picked up the Walkman off the sideboard and put it in the pocket of the steerhide jacket. I didnt even look back, just pulled the door as softly as I could then put the keys through the letter box.

It was sheeting rain and deserted streets but I was walking quick with the drops potting onto the steerhide jacket and the suitcase top. It was threeish on my watch.

When I got to the cash machine I used my card then checked the balance. He'd given me the inheritance from His father:

44,771.79

I started shaking my head with drips of rain coming down from the roof. I withdrew daily limit of £250. I looked round the deserted port with waves still whamming against the seawall.

At half five the Alginate early shift bus would take me out to the concession lands and I could wait for the Central Belt bus. Then a few days in London. I had over an hour to kill. I started climbing up Jacob's Ladder in the rain, up to the circular folly looking down on the port through the clouds of drizzle. You still couldnt see towards the pass where His village lay through the clouds.

W HEN I first returned to the resort I sat on the balcony of my hired apartment watching the changing light out at sea. I had supposed I would start waxing legs and bikini line when I moved to live there; then it dawned on me that you only wax to save time shaving them each morning and at last, Time was the one thing I had been able to buy: with firnickitiness I shaved them each morning.

It's proved nails grow quicker in summers and even for a while after youre dead. Not having the superstore work any more, my nails did brilliantly. In the mornings I'd use cuticle remover then push back and trim any hangnails.

For the first days, not wanting to miss a minute of the beautifulness of sunrises and sunsets, I sat on the balcony working on a suntan and putting basecoat on my fingernails. After an hour I'd just go and pick the basecoat off again, re-do them then peel the varnish off again, just for the feeling.

I used the harder side of emery boards on my toenails and had to leave the cuticle remover on much longer. I fitted my toe-dividers in then applied basecoat, two coats colour and a top coat to protect. I used the same varnish as for fingernails: the bronze plum and fuchsia.

All the time doing this there'd be music going on the brand new Sony HCD D109 music system I'd bought and had delivered. I got a free toaster, iron and hair dryer with it though it was too hot weather to use any of these.

Favourite CDs to listen to were rave stuff, FSOL's Room 208; Orbital and Computer Love by Kraftwerk. In the mornings I played Cucumber Slumber by Weather Report offof Mysterious Traveller or the title track offof Eno's Here Come The Warm Jets. I'd made a Sunshine tape on a C90 especially for the sunbathing sessions.

Track Listing:

SIDE A	*SIDE B*
Czukay Wobble Liebezeit: Full Circle.	Keziah Jones: Free Your Soul.
Zawinul: The Harvest.	Daniel Lanois: Still Water.
PM Dawn: So on & So On.	Spirit: Topango Windows.
Can: Pauper's Daughter & I.	John McCormack: Come my Beloved.
Scritti Politti: A Little Knowledge.	James Chance: Roving Eye.
Neville Brothers: With God On Our Side.	Hunters & Collectors: Dog.
Robert Calvert: Ejection.	Leisure Process: A Way You'll Never Be.
Hardware: 500 Years.	

The first few in-the-scud sunbathes on the balcony made my skin tingle. It brought up a right crop of little plooks in my pores, no bigger than the heads of common pins, across my shoulders and on thighs that the razor pushed away in the morning. After a week the reddish blotchiness where there'd been plooks got replaced by a rubbed bronziness then as I took the longer sunbathes the big golden tan started to rise through the moisturiser I plastered just all over me. After youve got the light tan it's a matter of keeping it with a few minutes every day. You must have a certain tan so you can go swimming for hours and dry on the beach. You have an all-over tan so's you can wear the real shorter stuff at the raves.

My body was so brown that a clutched glass in my hand made the palms look baby-pink and passing a mirror you noticed the milk I was drinking from a cup, all pale on my lips in contrast.

The path from my hired apartment to the beach front was like out the Bible under the fierceness of such sun. You followed the dust track past the Roman irrigation sluice, leading to the lemon and apricot trees. Behind the cypresses the goatherd was tap-tapping and the wee iron bells round the goats' necks clanged.

I stood still listening to the goat bells then took out the case and used the new lighter on a Sobranie Black Russian. I blew out rings of smoke. There was dust on my ankles. I stood on the one leg, licked saliva onto my finger then drew a wet clean line over the skin. Greyish dust stuck round a bubble of spittle.

Across the road I walked past each bar and restaurant on the curved promenade of palm trees till I stepped up on the terrace of the bar with chequered tables and chairs. That early every table was free under the warm awning. I lay my beach towel on the chequered chair so's my bare legs didnt get the feeling of next to plasticness. I put down my beach bag and sat keeping on the sunglasses.

The beach was already busy: families and holiday-makers, he-men in tight trunks, big old women in black one-piece swimsuits with their little grandchildren; you could see the other waitress who worked nights, topless, sleeping under a hired umbrella. Children formed a parade along the surf edge, running backwards and forwards as waves came in, the water carrying lifebelts and toys up towards the sandcastles getting built. Boys were thumping and diving over by the volley-ball net. Couples in pedalos were out beyond the point; a girl ran into the sea then fell on top her lilo.

I looked beyond the beach, staring at the sea and perfect horizon. The loveliness of that blue blemishless sky like a smooth fabric; the sharp blades of faraway yacht sails seemed to be drawing across and trying to slice into that fabric.

Without having to do the asking the waitress with the little mole brought me the usual breakfast. I nodded and smiled.

I drunk hot chocolate in the two gulps with a bite of

croissant between. The pastry was heavy and dampish from the microwaving, inside was a warm blob of chocolate. I sipped the orange juice, wolfed down the other croissant then I used my longer, sienna-painted nails to peel the orange. I popped segments in my mouth then used the new lighter on another Sobranie from the silver case.

When I snubbed out the butt you saw the loveliness of colours: my nails, the glittery gold Sobranie filter in the ashtray with the bright, tousled strips of orange peel among. I used the new lighter on another Sobranie cause of the alternative taste of smoke then orange.

You watched the holidaymakers in different stages of nudeness move along the promenade with slowness like they were trying to convince themselves they really were on holiday.

You saw a girl with an awkward-looking bottom but the face of an angel.

You saw the old couple come along the promenade, dressed in black and bent over so sharply they looked down directly on the tops of their sandals. They moved so slowly you kept checking the dark smudge of their further alongness then them coming back up, moving from palm tree to palm tree and pausing on the star shapes of shadow cast by the palm blades. Then they would shuffle on to the next tree and shelter from the sun there. Opposite me they stopped under shadow. The old lady separated from the man and turned her back to the low wall that stretched along the promenade. She sat down.

A big insect, a cicada, settled on the wall next to the old lady. She took off her sandal then with a manic energy swatted the heel down again and again pulverising the insect, all her old body jerking in the attack. Slowly she put the sandal back on, linked arms with the old man and they walked on.

After a bit the deaf man, his wee dog snapping at his ankles, stepped up onto the terrace. The doggy worried around, snarling in circles then was still when the deaf man pinned the leash under a chair leg and plonked himself down.

Without him having to do the asking the waitress moved to his table with a single bottle of beer and a tall glass on her tray. The deaf man waved at the sky and the waitress nodded, flipped the tray down by her leg then walked away past me smiling.

You saw the deaf man concentrate, pouring the beer down the inside of the slightly tipped glass, then he took a long sip and you saw his poorly shaved neck jumping as he swallowed, swallowed. You focused on the constellations of minute bubbles slipping back down the inside of the cold glass that was wet with condensation.

A strip of scorching sun was moving across my table, coming from a join in the awning above.

The deaf man piled small coins on the glass top of the table. The moment he left and moved down off the terrace the little doggy started snarling at his ankles; the deaf man moved his walking stick round, tap-tapping the dog who began gnawing and growling at the stick as they disappeared on up the promenade.

I left two thousands on the table then stood up. You felt the sun on you the second you were out from under the awning shade. I sat on the wall by the palm tree. I saw a train of ants were already carrying away bits of the shattered cicada. I took off my sandshoes and a tiny breeze moved the blades of the palm tree above.

Swinging the sandshoes in one hand I crossed the hot sand, stepping forward quickly it was so burny.

You choose a place as far as possible from any young men who plague the life out of you. I flicked away old fag butts with my toes, the reddishness of the nails showing up in the bright light with pale, almost whiteish-looking sand trickling offof them.

I spread the big towel and took stuff out my beach bag. I put Factor 12 on my nose and Factor 8 down my front, in general. I took off my bikini top, wiped my hands on it, threw it down by my legs and lay back. I checked my lipstick in the wee mirror and added a touch more. You noticed no other girls on the beach wore lipstick. I adjusted the earphones so I could hear the sunbathing tape better. I squinted out to the side, settling the Walkman inside the beach bag so's to protect it from the sun.

I took off the sunglasses and just lay with the sun battering down on me. With eyes screwed tight there was dark with fizzles of light then as I eased the eyes open a redness showed. The sun was this presence on the other side of the eyelids. When I opened my eyes a bit more, silvery crystals lingered about my lashes then I held my hand up and it blotted out the sun itself. I splayed my fingers out and the shelter of the shadow was on my eyes letting me study minutely my fingers and rings against the bluey height moving up forever above.

I gave myself twenty minutes front then I sat up and put the sunglasses on. I creamed Factor 8 down the back of legs and cupped some over my shoulders. I turned onto tummy and lay on the towel gritting teeth cause Factor 8 on front of the legs was pushed into grains of sand at the end of the towel. I hooked a finger under the bikini bottom and adjusted its position. I took off the sunglasses and lay my cheek on the towel, feeling the lumpy sand under. A layer of heat lay on top me. I started to sweat on my front. When I sat up and twisted round, sweat was between my bosoms and in a silvery patch round my belly. A layer of sand was stuck to my legs and I scraped the greasiness away with a nail leaving a clear line on the knee. You could see the little specks still under the skin: a pinkish one and a silvery but the tanned skin was making them disappear.

I squinted out to sea. I took the waterproof watch out the beach bag then put it on. I ran into the sea.

I swam for an hour, diving down so the water got colder then grabbing handfuls of sand offof the bottom. Right out at the buoys if you listened carefully you could make out the sound of cutlery crashing in the kitchens. I swam in and walked hunched forward with water dripping offof my face and lips. I bent down, picked up the bikini top then put it on. I stepped over the sand between sunbathers and holidaymaker families. Two guys stared at me in a plaguer way.

The two showers were up near the palm trees by the promenade. The showers were joined togetuer by the Tampax sign at the top. Pallet-like boards were under the two sprays where the sand was wet and shiny round them. An old lady with an amazing shape in a black costume was under a spray. A father was making two wee ones stand in the other spray. I waited.

Two girls about my age, brown as berries, were waiting behind me.

When the old lady moved away I got in under the spray. Fresh water was bouncing offof my face, running down my legs. The water stopped so I reached out an arm and pushed the plunger. The water started hitting, pouring down my front again. The tanned topless girls were together under the other spray almost next to me, turning their smiles under the jet of droplets. I leaned in and massaged my scalp.

When I'd got all the salty water rinsed out I walked back to my towel. Sand caked round my wet feet and water droplets fell from hair and finger-tips making little greyish coloured blots on the sand. I stood by my towel and squeezed out my hair making a splattering of craters. When I sat down on the towel my wet bikini bottom soaked through to the sand but the sun was already drying the drops clinging to my arms. I took off the watch and the bikini top.

I just sat in the sun drying. I put on more lipstick then used the new lighter on a Sobranie. After a good bit I put on sunglasses and bikini top, stood up and swung the leather beachbag over my shoulder then shook out the towel.

I walked up holding the two sandshoes and, sitting down on the wall, I used fingers to rub sand out from between my toes. When I pulled on the sandshoes you noticed all the ants had left of the insect was two wings that shimmered rainbowy colours.

I sat down in the cafe with the chequered chairs and without me having to do the asking the waitress brought me the Coca-Cola with ice and lemon in; spits of fizz from the glass caressed the back of my hand when I reached out for it. I looked straight at the horizon through my sunglasses.

Some wee ones came up off the beach for ice creams, when the waitress opened the top of the fridge you saw a cloud of condensation swirl a bit then fall.

I looked at the glass of Coca-Cola and took off my sunglasses. The ice in the drink was silvery at the top; where the ice cubes were thickest it lightened the brown and bronzey colours of the drink.

When you looked at the sky you saw how near the sun was paler diluted blueness but blueishness grew near the sea till both met at the horizon in a black thready line.

When there was just ice in the bottom of the glass I left a two hundred coin on the table and moseyed back up the dust path among the orchards. At the pomegranate tree where theres the sign in all different languages saying about the Roman irrigation sluice I used the new lighter on a Sobranie. I took the left path that takes you out by the building where my apartment is.

Up in the bedroom I lay back listening to the local radio station in the coolness. Then I got up and put Hallucination Engine by Material on the CD and had a lukewarm shower with my sunglasses on and the door open for as to the sounds.

When I was out the shower I plastered myself in moisturiser and to show off my nice brown neck I put hair up in a French roll. I stood in front the stereo where I could listen to the music and looked out towards the balcony and the beach beyond, after using the new lighter on a Sobranie.

I changed into one of the ravey tops from the trendy shop along by the harbour. I put on the black skirt and the new Nikes. I counted enough cash for the usual meal and the eight thousand for Spook Factory. Out on the landing after locking the door I fixed my keys onto the black cord of the stone-thing necklace. The keys touched cold against my collar bone.

Without me having to do the asking the waitress brought me the meal as per usual along with the last night's bit of wine still left in the cold bottle. I'd sat at the corner table by the pot plant.

Over in the sky the sun was lower, people were shaking out towels down on the beach. Indentations of feet in the sand cast little cups of shadow. As people left the beach its surface seemed all the more perfect.

Behind me there was the rumble of pool table balls as young guys with their T-shirts on came up offof the sand.

I nodded and smiled as the waitress put down the bowls of salad and bread. I ate all the olives one after the other from round the salad and lined up the stones on the side plate. I skinned the flesh from each olive with my two top front teeth so if you fished the olive out you could see the little square cuts on it. After I'd bitten off most of the flesh, my tongue passed the stone further back in my mouth where I rubbed the rest off. Then I sucked the stone with its sharp little ridge before popping it out on my hand and lining it up with the other stones.

I poured a glass wine for the alternative tastes of olives then wine.

The bits of capsicum were more fleshy and, as you bit, a tasteless juice came out. I more often than not put in a whole potato with the mayonnaise on, passing it from one side of the mouth to the other, getting the mayo off. The soft sides of the potato hit against my incisors. I was putting a potato after a bit of lettuce after a potato into my mouth and wolfing the lot down.

As per usual before the light got too poor the lone guy with the metal detector was the only person down there, patrolling the beach, sweeping the sand in front him.

The white dome of the lighthouse started pivoting round away up on the blunt point at the end of the plateau.

When people stopped on the promenade to lean in at

the menu, the electric bulb in the glass case lit their faces, like a mask.

Blue Blue Ocean by Echo & The Bunnymen was going up on the cafe sound system. I sighed and scraped the remainder lettuce onto my plate, then, using the fork I held the tomato and capsicum on the dish, letting the dressing run out: peacocks' eyes of olive oil skimming a-top the vinegar, dapples of black pepper and tawny streaks of mustard popped onto the biggest leaf of lettuce. I forked out the last potato salad then folded over the lettuce leaf holding it secure with the knife. The lettuce fibres cracked then I flattened it all with the side of the knife. I spiked a smeared tattie, layed it on the envelope of lettuce then pushed till the whole carry-on was fixed together. I opened my mouth and devoured the lot.

I tore out the doughy bit of the roll and took five swallows of the wine. I soaked up oil and dressing in the doughy bit and chewed it all round. I'd had ample.

You saved enough wine so you had a good glassful at the end of the eating for sipping along with a Sobranie and the alternative tastes.

You couldn't see the surf down in the darkness but you could hear it. Sometimes you saw the light of a fishing boat out in the bay.

A few families had come in while I was eating and I was the only one sitting alone on the terrace. I took five more wine swallows then a puff of Sobranie. You saw the girl with the face of an angel walk on the promenade and she'd got all dressed up. The lights of the restaurants and neon from the bars only stretched halfway down the sand.

It was younger groups of people starting sitting down at the tables round me. You couldnt understand any of the words going on at the tables. There was a pattern to the talk: one person's yabbers, the solo talker raising the pitch of voice seconds before then all round the table bawled out laughing. After that another talker began; some of the listeners had their legs crossed under the chequered tables, some fiddled with the plastic cocktail stirrers, propelling the ice round and round at the bottom of their empty glasses, then all the laughing and hysterics.

Sitting still and alone at my table the pattern of the talking fitted in with the rhythm of the water hushing down in the darkness. The noise of words was so meaningless it was restful, I was nodding off a bit.

Two silent older men were moving chess bits across a glass table top, not needing a board cause of the chequered pattern. When a family moved away from the table beside me it was two young men who manoeuvred from a further away table to beside me. I looked out at a fishing boat light on the black sea. The waitress crossed and took an order from the men next me. I caught her eye and handed her the money. Without waiting for change I stood up and walked out cause you could tell a plagueing was coming from those two. I moved along the curved promenade then I turned following the flicking strobe beacon through the darkened orchards.

At Spook Factory the bouncers stamped my arm and slid aside the metal door. You walked in through dry ice and dope smell. Parliament doing One Of Those Funky Things offof Motor Booty Affair was being played up on the big main dancefloor. People were eating burgers inside the two burned-out doorless cars in front the bar. I pointed to the big bin of mineral water bottles and handed over a five hundred coin.

I walked through to the rave catacombs down the curved corridors. You heard the trancey ambient getting louder. You pulled aside the curtain and stepped into the hot complete pitch darkness. You could tell it was DJ Sacaea: swirly bass patterns coming out the bins and dark-side fx getting fed in. You felt air, responding to bodies moving about quickly to the sounds in the blackness. You saw the orangey brightening then steadying tips of joints by the row of carpets and cushions behind the pillars.

The ship's horn honked telling us the lights were going to come up: there were topless girls in shorts and beads doing their thing to the music with guys wearing shorts and baseball caps. A couple were snogging or maybe even going dirty on each other, down on the cushions, it was difficult to tell what was going on even with the low lights up.

You saw people on their own, drinking Red Bulls and looking the same as me then the darkness came again after Sacaea sounded the ship horn.

A dreamy repeating pulse began. Immersed in the darkness, feet kept on the floor by the water bottle, bottom half followed the pulse and drone. Sometimes torso and arms were everything else: the bleepers or synth patterns; sometimes I stretched up fingers – my keys banging, banging against collarbone.

My hair was slapping about, it got so sodden with sweatness and the mineral water I'd tip over it every now and again. The way Sacaea was doing it the music was just a huge journey in that darkness. When we needed brought down to rest the ambient let us relax then he slowly built us up until we were back in hardcore again and he pushed the 'core as long as I could take it before much softer synth waves were beaming across us.

I'd lost my water bottle. Stretching up fingers to touch the ever-so-occasional laser needles you could feel how high up your legs the skirt might be with the pounding, pounding of hardcore all round you.

I was so close some boy or girl that their sweat was hitting me when they flicked arms or neck to a new rhythm. I slid my foot to the left. You felt the whole side of a face lay against my bare back, between shoulder blades. It was still part of our dance. If the movement wasnt in rhythm it would have changed the meaning of the face sticking there in the sweat. You didnt really have your body as your own, it was part of the dance, the music, the rave.

The face moved away then fingers touched my neck and I put my fingers on the cheeks to feel its maleness: bit beard. I leaned forward for the cuddle, our lower

halves were still moving fast to the rhythm. No judge-
ment: he couldnt know who I was. I wouldn't know him.
I took the kiss, my finger touched his wet curl of hair,
like a monocle hanging behind his ear. Having to do this
position to keep the kiss we stepped back and a flashing
arm caught my ear. The softness of wet bosom pressed
my elbow so I threw an arm round a girl and the three of
us danced in a link till the repeating pulse slowed and I
turned my head to kiss the male mouth all the deeper.
The male hand slid up and started to go a bit dirtyish on
me so I turned away then felt my way to the left. My
foot found the edge of the carpet but you couldnt tell if I
was on the near or far side of the room. I started moving
left but bumped a pillar then stepped on a leg of someone
then you saw the glow as a figure came through the
curtain by the air conditioning box. I squeezed between
two standing people.

In the curved corridor you saw sweat all up my legs.
My tummy that showed under the rave top was shiny and
violent-looking with sweat. A boy pushed out through the
curtain and we both glanced at each other in a wondering
way. I stepped down to the toilets. I went into a cubicle.
When I'd finished and stood you saw some talcum powder
specks on the dark seat from me. I smiled. I reeled off
some rough-feeling toilet paper and dabbed at the sweat.

Out in the corridor I looked back at the curtain then
the other way down past the fruit machines. I walked
down to where the guy was, by the Formula One
machine.

Trips? he says.

I just held out the money for one. He looked both ways then passed it into my hand. I'd swallowed it down before I was back at the curtain.

My ears were buzzing and the strobe flicked way back through the orchards but I passed the pomegranate tree then down onto the promenade. I strolled to the far end looking at late crowds all talking and laughing round the tables in the disco bars. At the far end I sat down on the wall beyond the flashing beer signs. I looked along the shore road to the buildings the woman with the south accent from the letting agency had showed me the day I picked the apartment.

I stood up and moved above the rocks. I saw the lighthouse on the end of the plateau turning round. Below me, among the rocks, old greyheads were fishing. Tall rods were stuck on holders fixed into the sand. The rods mustve had batteries in them somewhere cause right on the very tips, nodding in the darkness, were tiny greeny lights. Back a bit the fishermen had a gas camping lamp on a fold-out table with that pale ghostliness cast out round it. The three men were standing so close in to the glow you couldnt see faces. They were drinking from little glasses. You saw the rich reddy jewel of a wine bottle in front the light.

I turned and walked away. You heard crickets chirp-chirping in the scrub off between the summerhouses. I walked to the top of the long avenue where the buildings began. Ahead, lanterns were shining out a building to the right and showing across the pavement. There was silentness. I stepped into the glow. In silence about forty people were sitting round tables on an open veranda. There was such fright at living humans sitting in silentness you just stared. They were sat like people in the bars and restaurants and a waiter was crossing with a tray but there was no talking or laughing. Then you saw the cards. It was the bridge club. You could hear the sea wash way over the roofs of the houses. Some had started to look up at me staring so I walked on.

Further down I turned in between two darkened houses. As you passed scrub the crickets stopped rattling, then started up when behind. Way in front I saw froth as a small wave fell over in the sea. The noise of the falling wave moved way along to my right. There was pitch darkness between me and the wave. I screwed up eyes waiting for them to adjust then shuffled forward a bit.

There was a strip of this queer volcanic rock, small pools of water and roundish nodules of stone. It was like the coast had melted then gone hard again. During the day water mustve been trapped in hot sun, cause some wee pools gave off a pong.

You saw milky light across the smooth skulls and queer blobs of rock with bubble holes and arches drawing fine shadows. Moon had appeared above the vertical cliffs down the coastline.

My ankle skited away under me and I jabbed out a hand into the black: I was right there, by the water. I stood looking out to sea for a bit, the smear of moonlight coming towards. I looked round in the night, over the dark block of the faraway summerhouse. I pulled up the rave top; the keys and stone-thing necklace thumped down on my collar bone. I undid the zip on the skirt and flicked the button with my finger, holding the hem so's it wouldnt go and touch a stinky water pool. I stepped over the skirt with each foot then tugged off each Nike not undoing laces. I put a foot into sea.

Water reached my ankles but I stepped forward again and the leg sunk right in.

You had to stand still while the other foot edged forward feeling for something secure. I brought the foot up but then a small wave hit on the knees so I wobbled. In deeper water caused by the wave I felt kelp or seaweedy stuff shift against my shins. I went a bit shivery.

I cooried down on hunkers dunking my bottom and thighs under. Balancing with a hand on rock I felt out with one leg bent at the knee then my toes found flatness in front of me. When I put the other foot next it and stood, the water was up to the top of my legs. Another wave came in and you could sense by the pull and suck of the water it was deeper to my left so I stepped there. You could hear water pouring off a flat rise of rock behind me. I was getting all the deeper.

I walked forward. For a patch it seemed shallower then you felt a surge of real sea; my feet lifted a little then I swam forward. My heart was really pounding but the pull and tug pull and tug of water against something solid was gone from my shoulders; I pivoted my body down and already I was out of my depth. I started the night-swimming.

Further out I turned to try check my position. You could hear water on rocks; you couldnt see the lights of the restaurants, only moon above the sharp cliffs and moon splattered across the sea I was in. I let out a wee laugh, turned and swam on further out.

I went on my back and floated feeling the keys and stone of the necklace hanging at the back of my neck among hair, snaking and floating as part of the water movements, gently tugging my head backwards.

All was made of darknesses. My chest showed out the oily black surface. I angled my toes round so the moon was rising out right between my bosoms. I let the coldish surface of the water cluck around my ears so's I was looking straight up at the sky. Stars were dished up all across bluey nighttimeness.

I let my legs sink down; my nudeness below in the blackwater; legs hung in that huge deep under me and the layer on layer and fuzzy mush of star pinpricks were above with the little buzz of me in between.

I sucked in air deep and dived down sharply in the nightwater. I kicked once more, a wave of much colder water surrounded and a pressure was in ears. I jerked eyes open in the nothingness. Salt nipped as I seemed to be spinning slowly so I blew out to stop me rising and when my bubbles were gone, then there was silentness. My ears squeaked, I opened my legs wide, yanked my head back and threw out my arms to keep me down in those waves and layers of cold thick-seeming water. Suddenly there was a rumbling and the liquid slid offof me as I came to the surface: warm air on my face, the sounds of the earth and all under the moon.

I started the swimming in. You noticed how my heart was racing. I was swimming with faster and heavy sweeping pulls of arms. Once my cupped hand broke surface as I pulled back a stroke and it was the splash that sounded like panic. I hissed in a breath then kicked harder.

Something touched me on a bosom so's I rolled over and grunted out loud. My shoulder came against something with a sharp bump: rock. I found I could stand. I sputtered out and laughed. I walked forward, then when I was in up to the knees I bent forward taking breaths with hands on thighs.

I swayed from side to side moving among the queer-shaped stones doused in moon that reflected on my dark wet skin. The keys at my neck chinked.

I'd come ashore from the nightswimming further up the raised beach of volcanic rock. I saw the ravey top. I rubbed my hands on it then just tugged it over my neck. I put on the skirt and the Nikes. I shook my hair and pulled at it to see how fankled and sticky with saltiness it was.

The trainers squelched a little as I began picking my way over the lunar rocks towards the buzzing of crickets. I crossed to the opposite pavement but most of the bridge players had gone from the veranda.

I passed the fishermen then took the path up beside the cypresses and under the pomegranate tree. You saw the strobe of Spook Factory and, through the concrete skeleton of the unfinished apartment block, the lighthouse and the moon. Across the orchard there was something else. You could see part of a giant blue eye in pale light. I stepped into the lemon and apricot trees. You could see the top of the concrete screen at the late-night drive-in cinema.

Among the trees you became aware of the perfumes from the thick leaves that were black in those shadows where I stood.

The massive pale lips of a girl seemed to turn up to the night sky ready for kissing and you could see the light from the screen flicker on the leaves. I turned facing the sea. You heard a drip come offof my hair. I closed my eyes there in the quietness just breathing in and breathing in. I hadnt slept for three days so I could know every minute of that happiness that I never even dared dream I had the right.

ANOTHER DAWN found me moving through the ripe orchards. Black bats swooped above. The colours of the sky were busy changing as the dogs across the villa range barked to each other.

Piles of cloud sat out to sea jammed against the horizon and the first of the sun behind was all citrusy in the pine trees on the far point. The sun slid up over the mimosas till cloud out at sea started to curl and light fell in masses on the water; the bottom of a cloud bank broke away while a bar of sky was stained pinkish then the purple-like shadows changed into a peach roof above. At full light small pools of silver glistened on all the greenery. The bats were gone.

Circles of fallen oranges lay under the dark leaves of their tree. I shivered in the shade then reached up and twisted an orange from the tree. Further on I pulled another two oranges, cupping them in my arms with my long shadow out in front of me then when I looked up there was a burning bush blazing away ten feet in front. I dropped the oranges.

It was the sun behind me shining on the tree. The

beautiful blossom tree had been strangled to death under the mother of pearl psychedelics from a couple of thousand clinging snail shells.

I sneaked round staring then moved on quick to try and cross to the riverbed path but I misjudged or just couldnt after all the wastedness with raving so's I just went flying with my hand shooting out as I fell. My open palm hit stone and you felt the two long nails get forced back then snap as my glittering knee shuddered against the ground.

I got straight back up. Reddish soil was on my thigh. Pale bits of skin at the ball of the thumb were pushed up with mud round. Blood was rising out from the little blocks cut in the hand. Two of the fingernails were only just hanging so I shook them free and they fluttered to the soil.

A long snaking of blood was coming from a crossways slit on the glittering knee and you saw the trickle reaching the top of the Nike. I tried to smile and look straight ahead but white pin pricks of light were filling both eyes. I stepped forward with my cut hand stretched right out feeling a way through the trees but I was fainting at the sight of my own blood, rolling through explosions of white then the bass drum sound of me hitting the ground and lying still.

I saw an atlas of clouds linked in the sky and let out a chuckle that became a cough. I tried to get up slowly. I felt and the keys were at my neck. I was shaking and famished. I took some slow steps forward not looking down at the cut knee. Just a little longer. Please, I says out loud.

I moved past the irrigation sluice till I was under the tree. I held my head back and squinted up at it in the clear light. I was under the pomegranate tree. All fruits on branches were burst right open and the bright reddy insides had spilled out in the sun. Clumps of flies were feeding on the peeled-back, split skin and glistening flesh. It looked like little burst, mutilated creatures were up the pomegranate tree.

I was managing to make it to the end of the path near the pavement and the apartment building. As I turned out of the orchard something bright caught my eye. It was a scarlet speck moving over the dry earth by the irrigation sluice: it was one of my broken nails being carried away by ants.

THROUGH MY breath, brake lights bloomed up in the bitter cold night and the lift toot-tooted under the bridge taking the fort junction without indicating and away.

Soon as it was gone I stepped forward and burst ice in a muddy puddle tinkled together. I sucked in and held my breath: listening, listening.

Way up the railway track in the port direction you saw the dull light of the steamed-up signal box windows. In the other direction you saw the steady pattern of track leading away into the dark. The sleepers were pale with frost.

I put one hand on the fence then climbed over, jumping into the bushes despite the noise. I rushed down the steep embankment pushing an avalanche of cinders and frozen stiff dead leaves in front me.

I stopped at the bottom of the bank and peered both ways up the railway track. I turned and walked away from the signal box, into the darkness towards the pass. So's I couldnt be seen against the paleness of frozen sleepers I kept well to the side, walking just below where the stone ballast stuff was.

Further along the straight track my feet rung hollow

over the stream bridge. I looked over and there were big froths and cankers of ice in at the banks. I looked around me but there was no moon. I hoiked the haversack up more comfy on my back and moved to the middle of the track before walking on.

The sleepers were skiddy and too close together to step from one to the other but too far apart to step comfortable over three.

After about the mile I was entering the pass proper, and though you couldnt see, the sheep fanks were off above me. I followed the reverse curves to where the mountain's first slopes were up to the left.

A gust of bitter wind made me turn my head to the side both cause of coldness and to listen for an evening train.

I was well into the pass; the odd vehicle down the steep embankment went by and in headlights you saw the black water of the loch and shadows moved across the icy sleepers. Then I heard it.

A diesel accelerating away from the Falls platform where The Turbines Bar was, two miles on. I looked to the darkness where the road was then stepped down the bank being canny of any sudden drop but it wasn't too sheer.

I sat down resting the haversack against a trunk and wedging in my feet against the next one down. I was tired in the awful coldness and I shut my eyes.

I jerked awaker, I'd sort of done a wee nod off and the ground was shaking under my bottom, like the sand had under Couris Jean. The embankments trembled so's I pushed more into the tree trunk and lay legs flat against the soil. I was going to put my hands up to ears but just didnt. The engine started accelerating again before it got to me. It was really screaming and as I slowly turned my head you saw the diesel exhaust flame dancing up on the roof and the crack-cracking then the thumping of coach wheels with their lights stripping across me then the hiss of the end. I stood straight and in the darkness pulled myself up the embankment onto the track in time to see the red tail-light swing round the far corner.

I turned and walked on down the railway line. With the wind the only way to walk was hands in the steerhide jacket pockets, head down striding forward sometimes stumbling a bit on uneven ballast or once on some rail bits piled along the track. Then I walked in the middle of the track despite the slipperiness of sleepers, the awkward-nesses of their distance from each other for comfortable steps and the tendency to keep looking back in case a special train other than the usual evening-only should materialise.

I stopped walking, squinting my eyes through the trees.

I couldnt see the bulb way up ahead where the Falls platform used to be, or any lights at all down below where The Turbines Bar should have been.

I walked on squinting beyond where the viaduct should have been; still there was no light of any kind at the little unmanned station.

Out through the curls of hair on my shoulder you could see the headlights of another vehicle below.

I was a lot further down the line then cause I could see the shape of the Falls platform shelter across the viaduct. Yet there was no sound of the waterfall. I was right next it but there was only the wind moving the tops of trees on the lower part of the embankment.

I walked onto the first section of the short curved viaduct; I was screwing up my eyes into the dark as to what was wrong with the waterfall, then you saw.

The entire cliff and rocks had gone and frozen into a massive drooping wall of ice. Rows of icicles could be seen over the viaduct's walls, dangling into the darkness.

I gave a big shiver then crossed the rest of the viaduct, lay my hands down on the dark wood platform to bunk myself onto it and swung my legs round mankying the jeans up even more. I wiped my hands on their arse.

A ribbon shape moved across the dark water. It was smoke from the chimney of The Turbines Bar yet there were still no lights to be seen and it couldnt be near closing time. Although I'd walked about three mile from where the lift had dropped me off it couldnt possibly have taken that long.

I clung to the railing on the winding path down from the Falls platform to the main road. There was no light anywhere in the bar building, down in the power station carpark or across on the pontoon section where the main road crossed the sluices. I peered over where the tunnel entrance into the mountain is. I smelt some lovely wood smoke. I climbed up the steps to The Turbines Bar door. I hesitated outside then pushed it open.

A couple logs were blazing up under the big brass flue in the centre of the room and this was the only light-source in the bar. Long shadows and dark corners were everywhere with flame light flicking over the empty stools and corner booths.

Not a soul was there. I crossed to the square brickwork fire and warmed my hands. The door spring pushed it shut behind me. I peered in round the back of the bar and squinted into the shadows: nobody.

I got the haversack off and leaned it against the bar. I felt a definite gust of cold air from through the back. Then you heard a faint voice so's I edged through the lifted counter-hatch then poked my head in the rear area. There was a row of metal beer casks then you heard more voices. There was an open door to the outside. I moved over to it and looked out.

Standing with their backs to me were three figures that you couldnt quite make out. They were just standing but they seemed to be looking up the mountain above us. As my eyes adjusted you saw it was right enough. Two men and a younger girl were just stood there peering queerly up at the mountain in the darkness. You saw the man nearest me's breath.

Suddenly a man-voice goes, Must be heavy right enough.

Let's go back inside; it's freezing, goes a girl's younger voice in a south accent.

The man nearest me turned and I coughed.

Oh jesus!

Whos that? says another man-voice.

Sorry, I goes.

The three were staring at me a bit flabbergasted-looking; my hair mustve been quite a mess too.

The two men carried on staring at me but the girl who was stood at the rear squeezed past them cause they were standing on a concrete path with sort of embankment up to the height of their chests.

We've had a power cut, says the girl coming right up to my face, squinting at me.

Oh, I goes.

Eh, go on in or we'll all catch our death out here, says the girl.

Cause I was first one in line I had to turn and lead the way back in the door indian-file, past the metal beer kegs, into behind the bar then through the lifted-up hatch in the counter to stand on the correct side.

As we walked through I says, Sorry, I just sort of heard your voices; there were no lights on in the bar, I didnt know if you were open or what was happening.

The young girl moved to the till and you saw her checking it before she came over and stood beside the fire with me and the two men. You saw the men had the power station logo on their overalls. The baldier man coughed, clapped his hands together and says, Brass monkeys, eh?

Aye, I goes and nodded.

The man coughed again.

The less baldy nodded towards the top of the bar and went, Up there, way up there by the dam. It must be bad. The snow. It means there's heavy heavy snow when you get a short-out like this. Has to be bad to cut us off right here.

I nodded.

They'll have it going in half an hour, says the other man, looking at the girl, not me.

Aye, half an hour max, it's just a matter of them switching it over to back-up but someone'll need to go up in a four-wheeler to check the sub-station.

There was silentness. Total silentness cause there was no fridges or anything going. A bit of ember tinkled in the fire. I held out my fingers.

Hitching it? goes the guy next me, nodding to my haversack.

Aye. Sort of. Looking for work to be honest.

Work? went the girl.

Aye. Know anything going?

Phew, bad time of year; you qualified in anything, you a student or that? says the baldy.

Nut. I'll do anything though, I mean anything not in the port; I was wondering about the villages and how about yon superquarry, is that still on the go out the . . .

I'd forgot the word in the language for it then I remembered it.

. . . Out the peninsula? I goes.

The peninsula. The superquarry. Aye, aye it's still on

the go. You say *not* in the port. You dont want to work in the port? Youre sort of narrowing down your chances a bit there.

The less baldy says, Only jobs for lassies out the super-quarry is cleaners, theres two hundred men out there now but it's mostly going to be the older women that'll get that kind of work.

What about the Alginate factory? I goes.

Alginate? That shut down three year back. Are you from this way or something? went the baldy really looking at me.

I nodded then says, A good while back, aye. I've been travelling. Travelling round a bit.

There was more silence.

Baldy goes, Aye could be theres an ice problem, they have cameras at the outflow checking for blockages, trees and branches or that; they can light it up if they send divers down at night, the water's dumped from the dam down these tunnels inside the mountain, thousands of tons of water that turns the turbines then the water flows out into the loch at the end of that conduit. If the water levels in the dam get low we can pump water back up while it's the off-peak demand, at night.

Perfect, eh, the system'll last for eternity, it's all auto-mated, we just keep an eye on things.

Not tonight fellows, goes the girl.

We'd best shoot if they've got trouble down there, goes the other, swallowing the last from a cup of coffee that was sat somewhere out to his left in the shadow.

Right well, mind how you go, says the baldy one and coughed.

Bye bye pet, the other smiled at the girl.

The first one pushed open the door and as each stepped out they both peered up into the sky.

The girl collected two coffee cups from out the shadows and carried them to the bar.

Can I get you anything?

Ah, no thanks, I says.

She clinked the coffee cups into a sink or something that you couldnt see under the counter and says, Just as well it is not Saturday evening. With these beer pumps not working the power station fellows would all be onto shorts and go mad.

I smiled.

So youre from here then? she says, standing out in shadows so's I couldnt hardly see her.

Aye, I am.

Oh, where from?

The port.

Oh, I'm up here for my university research, a bit of extra cash always helps doesnt it?

Aye.

I'm an ornithologist.

Birds.

Yes. Eagles actually. Theres a nest site up on the corries above the dam and I'm part of a three-year project monitoring them.

Right enough? I goes.

Theyre probably up there circling above us now.

So do you live here? I says.

Yes. I've a flat up above.

Go into the port much?

Sometimes.

Is The Mantrap still there, the disco with the bakery under?

You didnt used to go there did you? A fellow got his ear bitten off there in the summer. Everyone I know goes to The Waterfront, it's really nice. The Mantrap's a scabby dump. So youre looking for work now are you; what were you doing before?

Travelling. Travelling round.

Did you get a lift here from one of the power station workers coming in to night shift?

No.

It's a funny place to ask to get dropped off out in the middle of nowhere.

I didnt get dropped here, I've been walking a bit.

It's terribly cold to be out walking in this weather, you should be careful.

Nothing'll happen to me, I says.

The girl held a open cigarette packet towards me.

I've given up, no thanks, I says.

I looked around and goes, Would there be any chance of crashing here the night, I've not much money or that.

She blew a noise out her mouth and goes, Well no, I mean I'm sorry but, well my uncle you see, he'll be here soon enough to empty the till and he'll be worried about the beer what with this power cut. I dont think he'd be eye to eye about me letting people stay over.

Your uncle?

Yes, he bought this place four years ago.

I see, I goes.

Yes, so I mean I'm really sorry. Listen I was thinking. My uncle's friend has a hotel; chalet style, out at the airstrip on the island.

The island? I went.

Yes. By the airstrip. I mean if you tried there I'm sure he may still be looking for staff.

I'll keep it in mind. Look would there be any chance of a lift with any of the power station crew, out to one of the villages or that?

Well the night shift's on, just those two skivers are always last in. The shift doesnt finish till after four.

Ach, it doesnt matter, I says, hoisting the haversack.

If you hitch along the road now theres bound to be a few cars going out to the villages at this time.

Aye, bye now, I says.

Outside in the coldness I got the CD Walkman, put it in the pocket of the steerhide jacket and set He Loved Him Madly going. I zipped the jacket and hands in pockets moved up to the road.

Headlights coming over the pontoon section were glaring in my face but without taking my thumb out the pocket I just turned my face aside, away from the glare. You heard the low gears, the shadows were swelling, the car revved by, the exhaust smoke pink in tail-lights. There was mistiness along the loch. You saw the tail-lights move down the shoreside road, headlights picking out some larches on one of the islets.

I took the dark path back up to the Falls platform and jumped down into the middle of the railway track. I kept walking on down the long straight forcing myself not to look backwards; just the music in my ears.

After a good bit I looked up and there seemed to be a feather coming down to me out the night so's I says out loud, Eagles, over the music sound.

It was the first snowflake twirling down. I held my face downwards but the big flakes just started settling on my hair, piling out the night onto me. I kept moving forwards though the snow was starting to fill the spaces between the sleepers under my feet. I knocked flakes out my hair but it made my fingers too perished.

I snorted out flakes that were smothering round my mouth then tried to shove my hands deeper in pockets. I shook my head and grogged back the first sob. I held my head back to try and clear my breathing but tickly snow settled on the closed eyelids. I wiped the worn steerhide sleeve across my nose with a sniff then swung my back round to the driving snow rushing in off the loch.

I walked on under the dark and whitenesses of such active skies. A white swarm of flakes was whirling in a confused way under the arched bridge so the only real shelter was right in the middle of its short length and if a train came growling round there would be no refuge but I leaned forward and stood there a bit.

I walked on till the track was beside the loch's level round the long curve. When He Loved Him Madly finished you heard the wavelets and you could see curved branches of driftwood that snow was stuck on.

In a queerly familiar way the looming things ahead were starting to take shape through the blizzard.

First thing you saw was, the sticking-up tower of the closed hotel then the shapes at the bottom of the steps. I knew where the steps were in the dark. I put my palm on the snow and jumped up on the platform. At the top of the stairway I looked up to the tower but the snow was too thick to see the whiteness of the top. There were no lights anywhere in the sleeping village.

I squinted up through the streaks of snowfall towards the pylons then I moved over into the lee of the hotel building. Through a window I could make out shapes inside, covered with white sheets and up on a wall a glass case with a big salmon shape in.

I quickly crossed the snowy road. It didnt have one set of vehicle tracks in it.

From the model I remembered the route across the graveyards but there'd been changes. Through the snow I felt the rise and fall of new graves under my feet.

I moved up the path towards the higher ground then started running when I saw the snow-covered hump of the Tree Church, kicking up sprays and shaking hair as I stepped into its shelter.

My movements sounded dense. Heavy snow was lay-ered on the evergreen roof, insulating the place. I lit the last lighter and held it up so shadows shook on the thatch of twigs above, then I moved deeper into the darknesses. A few steps down the aisle I put out the lighter then did a genuflection. Snow was whirling in around the window holes of the withered arbour but the front bench was sheltered. I did my prayer there then I blew on my fingers.

I got the backpack off and changed out of the wet socks into the last dry ones. When I sat crossways on the bench, I covered my tummy with the spare jumper. I was doing the shaking and my breath showed in the bitter coldness. After a good spell the shakes eased.

I lit the lighter and lifted up the big notebook. I had to grip the pen good and tight while writing a few sentences, then when it got burny-hot I put the lighter out.

I must have begun to doze off till I jerked awake and my feet shot out. I turned aside and all sicked up on the church floor.

After a bit my head started to nod-nod forward. Then I felt the icy cold drop on my scalp. Then another. One dripped down my cheek and brought me round. I felt less poorly. I put out my tongue and a lovely freezing drop landed there. I swung feet down and, missing the sick, I stood up straight.

The snow was thawing and drops of melty water were falling through the thatched roof making me better. I tidied up, managed the backpack on then stepped outside.

The moon was out. You could hear the plocking of

drips coming from the trees and you saw the snowy roof of the hotel below then there was a loud click and a hum. It came from the box up on the small pylon.

Down in the darkened village, lights went on behind some windows and the streetlamps juddered out pink haloes as they came to life. You saw the lights of the next village do the same, far across the concession lands.

I placed both hands on my tummy at the life there, the life growing right in there. The child of the raves.

I put my head down and closed my mouth. I started the walking forwards into that night.

ACKNOWLEDGEMENTS

Thanks to everyone who has helped me, especially Patsy and Frank Warner, and Cairns Leslie.

Some portions of this novel first appeared in *Northwords* magazine.